"You don't want to take me straight upstairs and make love?" Luca demanded. "You want *tea?*"

"Well, you've been traveling all day—"

His eyes narrowed with irritation. What kind of greeting was this? "You know, an Italian woman would never treat her lover so," he observed.

Slowly, Eve turned around. "Then I suggest you find yourself an Italian lover, instead of an English one."

Eve felt sick, and the sickness reminded her of the secret—such a tiny secret at the moment—which was growing inside her belly. Suddenly she realized that her instinct had been correct all along, and there wasn't any such thing as a "right time" to tell him.

Eve's nerve suddenly failed her. "I'll just finish making the tea," she blustered.

Still he watched and waited.

Eve tipped boiling water into the teapot, making a drink she knew neither of them would touch.

"I'm pregnant."

Born in west London, **SHARON KENDRICK** now lives in the beautiful city of Winchester in the U.K. and can hear the bells of the cathedral ringing out while she works. She has had zillions of jobs, which include photographer, nurse, waitress and demonstrator of ironing board covers. She drove an ambulance in Australia and appeared on television in Tehran, but writing is the only job she's had that feels just right. Her passions are many and varied, but include music, films, books, cooking, gazing at the sky and drifting off into daydreams while she works out passionate new love stories!

THE ITALIAN'S LOVE-CHILD

SHARON KENDRICK

PREGNANCIES OF PASSION

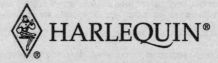

HARLEQUIN®

TORONTO • NEW YORK • LONDON
AMSTERDAM • PARIS • SYDNEY • HAMBURG
STOCKHOLM • ATHENS • TOKYO • MILAN • MADRID
PRAGUE • WARSAW • BUDAPEST • AUCKLAND

For the *charmant* Laurent Droguet, who not only has the
most dazzling smile, but also the most wonderful friends

ISBN-13: 978-0-373-82038-2
ISBN-10:   0-373-82038-0

THE ITALIAN'S LOVE-CHILD

First North American Publication 2006.

www.eHarlequin.com

Printed in U.S.A.

CHAPTER ONE

Eve saw him across the other side of the room and her world stood still. It was like watching a film, where fantasy took over and made real life fade away and it had never happened to her before.

That click. That buzz. That glance across the room which held and hung on in glorious disbelief as you met the eyes of a man and somehow knew that he was 'the one'. But of course it was fantasy, it must be—for how on earth could you see someone for a minute or a second and know that this total stranger was the person you wanted to spend the rest of your life with?

Except that this man was not a total stranger, though maybe that was fantasy, too. After all, it had been a long time.

She quickly glanced down at her drink and pretended to examine it, before risking another look, only this time he had turned away, and although her heart lurched with disappointment that he obviously didn't share her fascination, at least it gave her the chance to study him without embarrassment.

She was almost certain he was Luca, but he was certainly Italian; he couldn't have been anything else. Jet-dark hair framed the head he held so proudly and she drank in his perfect features as if trying to memorise them. Or remember them. The hard, intelligent black eyes, the Roman nose and an autocratic mouth which was both luscious and cruel.

5

He was striking and innately sexy, with a careless confidence which drew the eye and made it stay. In a room full of rich, successful men he stood out like some beautiful, exotic creature—his golden-olive skin gleaming like softly oiled silk, his body all packed, tight muscle. He looked like the kind of man who would command without even trying—an arrogant aristocrat from another age, yet a man who was essentially modern.

Eve was used to assessing people quickly, but her eyes could have lingered on him all evening. He wore his clothes with elegant assurance—a creamy shirt which hinted at a sinewed body beneath and dark, tapered trousers emphasising legs which were long and hard and muscular. He was very still, but that did not mask some indefinable quality he had, some shimmering vibrancy, which made every other man in the room fade into dull insignificance.

He had slanted his head to one side, listening to a tiny blonde creature in a sparkling dress who was chatting to him with the kind of enthusiasm which suggested that Eve wasn't alone in feeling a gut-wrenching awareness that she was in the presence of someone out of the ordinary. But why should that surprise her? A woman would have to be made out of stone not to have reacted to that package of unmistakable, simmering sensuality.

'Eve?'

Her reverie punctured, Eve turned her head to see her host standing beside her, holding a bottle of champagne towards her almost-empty glass. 'Can I tempt you with another drink?'

She hadn't been planning to stay long and she had intended her first drink to be her last, but she nodded gratefully, welcoming the diversion. 'Thanks, Michael.'

The drink fizzed into the flute and she glanced around the room. The blinds had been left open, but with a view like that you would never want to draw them. Moonlight and starlight dipped and dazzled off the lapping water outside and the excited chatter, which had reached fever-pitch, gave all the indications of this being a very successful evening indeed.

She raised her glass. 'Here's to birthday parties— your wife is a very lucky woman!'

'Ah, but not everyone likes surprises,' he said.

Eve's eyes strayed once more to Luca. 'Oh, I don't know,' she said slowly as her heart began to bang against her ribcage. 'Great party, anyway.'

Michael smiled. 'Yeah. And great you could make it. Not everyone can boast that they have a television personality at their party!'

Eve laughed. 'Michael Gore! You've known me since I was knee-high to a grasshopper! You've seen me with grazed knees in my school uniform.' She gave him a wry smile. 'And I hardly think that presenting the breakfast show on provincial television classifies me as anything as grand-sounding as "television personality".'

Michael smiled back. 'Ah, but the girl's done good,' he said.

Maybe the girl *had*, but right then she felt as vulnerable as that schoolgirl with grazed knees. And, to her horror, she realised that she had gulped most of the drink down and that Luca—if indeed it *was* Luca—was still listening to the animated blonde. And that the last thing she needed in her life was the complication of a charismatic, complicated kind of

man who was every woman's dream. Eve had learnt
early in life that it was important to have goals, just
so long as you kept them realistic.

'And the girl needs her sleep,' she sighed. 'Getting
up at three-thirty every morning tends to have a neg-
ative effect on your long-term energy reserves. You
won't mind if I slip away in a while, Michael?'

'I will mind very much,' he teased. 'But not if
your legion of fans are going to blame us for deep,
dark shadows under your eyes! Go when you like—
but why not come back for lunch again tomorrow,
when the show's over? There will be stacks of stuff
left and Lizzy and I have hardly had a chance to talk
to you all evening.'

Eve smiled. It would give her the opportunity to
play with her god-daughter who had been tucked up
in the Land of Nod all evening. 'Love to,' she murmured. 'About twelve?'

'See you at twelve.' He nodded.

She was tempted to ask him what Luca was doing
there, but she was not a guileless teenager now—and
what could she say, even if she was being her most
casual and sophisticated? Who's the man talking to
the blonde? Or, Who's the tall, dark, handsome
hunk? Or even if she plucked up courage to say, Is
that Luca Cardelli, by any chance?—all those would
make her sound like a simpering wannabe!

But maybe Michael had seen her eyes straying
over to the dark, still figure.

'You know Luca Cardelli, don't you?' he asked.

'Vaguely.' She gave it just the right amount of
consideration and kept her voice casual. 'He was
here one summer, about ten years ago, right?'

'Right. He sailed on a big white boat,' said

Michael, and sighed. 'Absolutely beautiful. Wonderful sailor—he put the rest of us to shame.'

Eve nodded. 'I didn't know he was a friend of yours?'

Michael shrugged. 'We were mates that summer and we've kept in touch, though I haven't seen him for years. But he emailed to tell me he was in London on business, and so I invited him down.'

She wondered how long he was staying, but she didn't ask. It was none of her business and it might send out the wrong message. There would be enough women here tonight fighting to get to know him, if the body language of the blonde was anything to go by.

'Oh, look—someone's setting off fireworks!' she murmured instead as in the distance the sky exploded into fountains of scarlet and blue and golden rain, and luckily Michael went to refuel someone else's glass, giving her the opportunity to go and stand by the window and watch the display, alone with her thoughts and her memories.

Luca watched her, at the way her bottom swayed against the silky green material of her dress as she walked towards the window. People were covertly watching her and he wondered why. But he had noticed her before that, even before she had started staring at him, and then pretending not to, but then, that was nothing new.

He had grown up used to the lavish attention of women right across the age spectrum ever since he could remember. He didn't even have to try and sometimes he wondered what it would be like if he did. The most rewarding business deals he had pulled off had been the ones he had really had to fight for—but women weren't like business deals.

He had been born with something which attracted the opposite sex like bees to honey and, when he had reached the age of noticing women, had quickly discovered that he could have whoever he wanted, whenever he wanted and on whatever terms he wanted. Very early on, he had learned the meaning of the expression, 'spoiled for choice'.

'Luca!'

He narrowed his eyes. The tiny blonde was pouting. He raised a dark eyebrow. 'Mmm?'

'You haven't been listening to a word I've been saying!'

She was right. 'Sorry.' He smiled, gave an expansive shrug of his broad shoulders. 'I feel guilty. I have been monopolising you, when there are so many men here who would wish to speak to you.'

'You're the only man I want to talk to!' she declared shamelessly.

'But that is unfair,' he responded softly. '*Sì?*'

The blonde wriggled her shoulders. 'Oh, I just love it when you speak Italian,' she confided.

He stared down into the widened blue eyes—deep and blue like a swimming pool and just begging him to dive in. Unconsciously, she snaked the tip of her tongue around her parted lips, so that they gleamed in invitation. It was almost too easy. She could be in his bed within the hour. At twenty-two, he would have been tempted. A decade later and he was simply jaded.

'Will you excuse me?' he murmured. 'I must make a quick telephone call.'

'To Italy?'

'No, to New York.'

'Gosh!' she exclaimed, as if he had proposed communication with Mars itself.

He smiled again, his mouth quirking a touch wearily at the corners. 'It was delightful to meet you.'

He made his escape before she asked the inevitable. How long was he staying? Would he like her to show him around? Unless she was bold enough to replicate the incredible time he had met a woman and within two minutes she had asked him to take her to bed!

The woman in green was still gazing out of the window and there was something intriguing about her stillness, the way she stood alone, part of the party and yet apart from it. Like a woman secure in her own skin. He made his way across the room and stood beside her, his eyes taking in the last rainbow spangles of the fireworks, set against the incomparable beauty of the sea.

'Spectacular, isn't it?' he murmured, after a moment.

She didn't answer straight away. Her heart was beating hard. Very hard. Funny how you could react to someone, even if you told yourself you didn't want to. 'Utterly,' she agreed, but she didn't move, didn't turn her head to look at him.

Now he was a little intrigued. 'You aren't enjoying the party?'

She did turn then, for it would have been sheer rudeness to have done otherwise, mentally preparing herself for the impact up close of the dark, glittering eyes and the sensual lips and it was as devastating as she remembered, maybe even more so. At seventeen you knew nothing of the world, nor of men—

you thought that men like Luca Cardelli might exist in droves. It took a long time to realise that they didn't, and that maybe that was a blessing in disguise. 'Why on earth should you think that?'

'You're here all on your own,' he murmured.

'Not any more,' she responded drily.

His dark eyes glittered at the unspoken challenge. 'You want me to go away?'

'Of course not,' she said lightly. 'The view is for free, for everyone to enjoy—I shouldn't dream of claiming a monopoly on it!'

Now he was very intrigued. 'You were staring at me, *cara*,' he observed softly.

So he had noticed! But of course he had noticed—it was probably as much a part of his life as breathing itself to have women staring at him.

'Guilty as charged! Why, has that never happened to you before?' she challenged mockingly.

'I don't remember,' he mocked back.

She opened her mouth to say something spiky in response, and then pulled herself together. He had been sweet and kind to her once, and just because a girl on the brink of womanhood hadn't found that particularly flattering, you certainly couldn't blame *him*. It wasn't *his* fault that he was so blindingly gorgeous and that she had cherished a schoolgirl crush on him which hadn't been reciprocated. And neither was it his fault that he was still so gorgeous that a normally calm and sensible woman had started behaving like a spitting kitten. She smiled. 'So what do you think of the Hamble?'

'It isn't my first visit,' he mused.

'I know.'

'You *know*?'

'You don't remember me, do you?'

He studied her. She was not his type. Tall and narrow-hipped where he liked his women curvy, and soft and small. Her face was not beautiful either, but it was interesting. A strong face—with its intelligent grey-green eyes and a determined mouth and soft shadows cast by her high cheekbones.

It was difficult to tell what colour her hair was, and whether its colour was natural, since she had caught it back severely from her face, and tied it so that it fell into a soft, silken coil on the base of her long neck. Her dress was almost severe too, a simple sheath of green silk which fell to her knees, showing something of the brown toned legs beneath. The only truly decorous thing about her was a pair of sparkly, sequinned sandals which showed toenails painted a surprisingly flirtatious pink, which matched her perfect fingernails.

He shook his head. 'No,' he said. 'I don't remember you. Should I?'

Of course he shouldn't. 'Not really.'

She gave a little shrug and turned her head to the view once more, but he put his hand on her bare arm and sensation shivered over her.

'Tell me,' he murmured.

She laughed. 'But there's nothing to tell!'

'Tell me anyway.'

Eve sighed. Why the hell had she even brought it up? Because she liked things straightforward? Because the probing nature of her job made her explore people's feelings and reactions?

'You came here one summer, a long time ago. We met then. We hardly knew each other, really.'

Luca frowned for a moment, and then his face

cleared. So it had not been a woman he had bedded and forgotten. There had been only one woman during that long, hot summer and she had been the very antithesis of this keen-eyed woman with her scraped-back hair. 'Unfortunately, *cara*, I am still none the wiser. Remind me.'

It had been a summer of making money, which had never really been in abundance in Eve's life. Ever since her father had died, her mother had gone out to work to make sure that Eve never went without, but there had never been any surplus to buy the things that seventeen-year-old girls valued so much in life. Dresses and shoes and music and make-up. Silly, frivolous things.

Eve had been overjoyed to get the summer job as waitress at the prestigious yacht club. She had never been part of the boating set—with their sleek boats and their quietly expensive clothes and all-year tans and glamorous parties. She'd had precisely no experience of waitressing, either, but she'd been known and liked in the village for being a hard-working and studious girl. And she'd suspected that they'd known she'd actually *needed* the money, as opposed to wanting the job in order to pick up a rich boyfriend.

And then Luca Cardelli had anchored his yacht one day, and set every female pulse in the vicinity racing with disbelieving pleasure.

The men who had sailed had been generally fit and muscular and bronzed and strong, but Luca had been all these things and Italian, too. As a combination, it had been irresistible.

She had been breathlessly starstruck around him, all fingers and thumbs, her normal waitressing skills deserting her, completely dazzled by his careless

Italian charm. On one embarrassing occasion, the plate of prawns she had been carrying had slipped so that half a dozen plump shellfish had slithered onto the floor in a pink heap.

Biting back a smile, he had handed her a large, linen napkin.

'Be quick,' he murmured. 'And no one will notice.'

No one except him, of course. Eve wished that the floor could have opened up and swallowed her. But she told herself it was just a phase in her life, of being utterly besotted by a man who saw her as part of the background.

Their conversation was limited to pleasantries about wind conditions and her uttering unmemorable lines such as, 'Would you like some mayonnaise with your salmon?' which made his act of generosity so surprising that she read all the wrong things into it.

The end-of-season yacht club ball was the event of the year, with the ticket prices prohibitedly high, unless you got someone to take you, and Eve had no one to take her.

'You are going dancing on Saturday?' Luca questioned idly as he sipped a drink at sundown on the terrace one evening.

Eve shook her head as she scooped up the discarded shells from his pistachio nuts. 'No. No, I'm not.'

He lifted a dark, quizzical eyebrow. 'Why not? Don't all young women want to dance?'

She ran her fingers awkwardly down over her apron. 'Of course they do. It's just…'

The brilliant black eyes pierced through her. 'Just what?'

Humiliating to say that she had no one to take her, surely? And not very liberated either. And the tickets cost more than she earned in a month. She wished he wouldn't look at her that way—though what way could he look for her not to feel so melting inside? Maybe if he put a paper bag over his head she might manage not to turn to jelly every time he was in the vicinity. 'Oh, the tickets cost far too much for a waitress to be able to afford,' she said truthfully.

'Oh.' And his eyes narrowed.

Nothing more was said, but when Eve went to fetch her coat that evening there was an envelope waiting for her and inside it was a stiff, gold-edged ticket to the dance. And a note from Luca. 'I want to see you dance,' it said.

Eve went into a frenzy. She was Cinderella and Rockerfella combined; it was every fairy tale come true. She borrowed a dress from her friend Sally, only Sally was a size bigger and they had to pin it into shape, but even after they had done it still looked like what it was. A borrowed dress.

Eve surveyed herself doubtfully in the mirror. 'I don't know.'

'Nonsense! You look gorgeous,' said Sally firmly. 'You definitely need some make-up, though.'

'Not too much.'

'Eve,' sighed Sally. 'Did or did not Luca Cardelli give you a ticket? Yes? Well, believe me—no man splashes out that much if he isn't interested. You want to look sophisticated. Mature. You want him to whisk you into his arms and dance the night away, don't you? Well, don't you?'

Of course she did.

But Eve felt like a fish out of water when she walked into the glittering room, feeling an outsider and knowing that she *was* an outsider. Everyone else seemed to be *with* someone, except for her.

And then Luca arrived, with a woman clinging to his arm like a limpet, a stunning vision in a scarlet dress that was backless and very nearly frontless.

She remembered almost everyone's eyes being fixed with envious fascination on them as they danced in a way which left absolutely no doubt about how they intended to end the evening and Eve felt sick and watched until she could watch no more. He said hello to her and told her that she looked 'charming'. It was a curiously unflattering word and she wondered how she could have been so stupid.

She crept home and scrubbed her face bare and carefully took off Sally's dress and hung it in the wardrobe. Luca left for Italy soon after and she didn't even see him to say goodbye. She didn't even get the chance to thank him.

But that experience defined her.

That night she vowed never to make her ambition overreach itself. To capitalise on what she was and not what she would like to have been. And she was no looker—certainly not the kind of woman who would ever attract a man like Luca Cardelli. She had brains and she had determination and she would rely on those instead.

Time shifted and readjusted itself, and it was an altogether different Eve who looked into the dark eyes with their hard, luminous brilliance.

Well, here it came, in a fanfare, with a drum roll!

'I was a waitress,' she said baldly, but smiled. 'At the yacht club.'

He shook his head. 'Forgive me, but—'

'You bought me a ticket for a dance.'

Something stirred on the outskirts of his mind. A hazy recollection of a sweet, clumsy girl who was trying to look too old for her age. His eyes widened ever so slightly. How little girls grew up! He nodded slowly. 'Yes. I remember now.'

'And I never got the chance to thank you. So thank you.' She smiled, the brisk, charming smile she used to such great effect in her professional life.

'You're welcome,' he murmured, thinking how time could transform. Was this sleek, confident woman really one and the same person?

His dark eyes gleamed and suddenly Eve felt vulnerable. And tired. She didn't want to flirt or make small talk with him—for there was still something about him which spelt danger and unobtainability. A gorgeous man who was passing through, that was all, same as last time. Stifling a yawn, she glanced at her watch. 'Time I was going.'

Luca's eyes narrowed in surprise. This was usually *his* line and never, *ever* had a woman yawned when he had been talking to her—not unless he had spent the previous night making love to her. 'But it's only nine o'clock.' He frowned. 'Why so early?'

'Because I have to work in the morning.'

'I am not sure that I believe you.'

'That, of course, is your prerogative, Mr Cardelli,' she returned sweetly

He stilled. 'So you remember my surname, too?'

'I have a good memory for names.'

'Unlike me.' He glittered her a smile. 'So you had better remind me of yours.'

'It's Eve. Eve Peters.'

Eve. It conjured up a vision of the first woman; the only woman. It was a small, simple and yet powerful name. It spoke of things lush and coiling. Of a fallen woman, driven by lust and the forbidden. He wanted to make a mocking joke about serpents, but something in those intelligent eyes stopped him. 'So what kind of job gets you up so early, Miss Peters? You're a nurse?' he guessed. 'Either that, or you milk cows?'

Eve laughed in spite of herself. 'Wrong!' She didn't want to be charmed by him, or made to laugh by him. She wanted to get away and she wanted it now. He unsettled her, made her feel like the woman she wasn't. She liked to be in control. She was calm, and considered and logical, and yet right now she was having the kind of fantasy which was more suited to the naïve adolescent she had abandoned that night along with the borrowed dress. Wondering what it would be like to be in Luca Cardelli's arms and to be made love to by him.

The filmy cream shirt meant that she could faintly see the whorls of hair which darkened the tight, hard chest and for one wild and crazy moment she imagined herself pressed against him, the strong arms enfolding her in a magic circle from which no woman would ever want to escape.

Luca saw her green-grey eyes momentarily darken and he felt an unexpected answering ache. 'Don't go,' he urged softly. 'Stay a little while and talk to me.'

His body had tensed and a drift of raw, feral male

scent began to intoxicate her. 'I can't,' she said, with a smile she hoped wasn't weak or uncertain. She put her glass down on the window-ledge. 'I really must go.'

'That, of course, is *your* prerogative,' he said mockingly.

Her resolve was beginning to fail her. 'Goodbye,' she said. 'It was nice to see you again.'

'*Arrivederci, cara.*' He stood and watched her weave her way through the room, his face giving nothing away. And maybe the blonde had been watching, for she reappeared by his side, looking like a tiny, overstuffed cushion in comparison to Eve's slender height and suddenly her simpering presence was cloying and not to be endured.

'I thought you were going to make a phone call, Luca,' she pouted.

Did she spend her whole life pouting? he wondered with a faint air of irritation.

'I was distracted,' he drawled. 'But thank you for reminding me.'

It hadn't been what she had meant to happen at all, and the blonde's mouth fell open in protest, but Luca had gone, pulling his mobile phone out of his pocket, and he went to stand outside, for privacy and for a better signal.

And better to watch the shadowy figure of Eve Peters as she walked down the path with the moonlit water dappling in the soft night air behind her.

CHAPTER TWO

EVE knew that people thought that working in television was glamorous, but people were wrong. Waking up at three-thirty had never been easy and the following morning was no exception, made worse by a foul, chill wind blowing in, which had the kind of drizzle which could turn the straightest hair into a frizzy cloud.

On automatic pilot, she showered and drank strong black coffee, and when the car arrived to collect her to take her to the studio she sat in the back with the newspapers as usual, only for once it was hard to concentrate on the day's news.

The truth was that she had had a disturbed night and that it had been disturbed by Luca Cardelli. He had burst into her dreams like a bright, dazzling meteorite, his brilliant black eyes mocking her and tantalising her and making her feel that she had missed an opportunity by leaving the party early.

But dreams were curious and capricious things, and unlike life you had no control over them. All he had done was to awake something in her subconscious, some forgotten teenage longing which had never quite gone away.

And dreams were soon forgotten. They weren't real. Neither was the ridiculous fluttery feeling she felt at the base of her stomach when she thought of him and there was a simple solution to *that*. She tried her best not to think of him but he stubbornly stayed on her mind.

She wished now that she had asked Michael how long he was here for—but surely it would be a flying visit? His life wasn't here, was it? His life was in Italy—a different, unknown life in a country as foreign to her as he was.

That morning's show contained the usual mix of items, including a dog which was supposedly able to howl in time to the national anthem. Unfortunately, the animal refused to perform to order—the poor thing cowered and was terrified and then was sick in a corner of the studio. Johnny, her co-host, threw a complete wobbly afterwards, and Eve was relieved to get away after the post-show breakdown.

The car dropped her off just after eleven and she closed the door of her tiny cottage with a sigh of relief. She went upstairs, wiped off all her heavy studio make-up, stripped off her clothes and took a long, hot shower, blasted her hair dry and knotted it into one thick plait.

Feeling something close to human again, she put on a pair of black jeans and a charcoal-grey sweater, aware that she would have grubby little fingers crawling all over her, then set off for Michael and Lizzy's, stopping off on the way to buy a colouring book and some crayons for Kesi.

She rang the bell and Lizzy answered it, a look of repressed excitement on her face, as though the party were just about to happen, rather than having taken place the night before.

'Eve! You look gorgeous!'

'No, I don't. No make-up and slouchy old jeans.'

'Well, you looked pretty amazing on the box this morning!'

'Ah, but that's the magic of the make-up artist. Did you see the sick dog?'

'*Did* I? Michael recorded it for me. Poor thing! Come on up. He's taken Kesi out, but he shouldn't be too long.'

'And how *is* my gorgeous little god-daughter?' asked Eve as they walked into the bright, first-floor sitting room. 'I thought—' But what she had been thinking flew completely out of her mind, for sprawled on one of the long sofas, reading a news-paper, was Luca Cardelli.

He glanced up as they entered and his dark eyes glittered with what looked like mischief, but under-pinned with something else, something which Eve couldn't quite work out. Something which made her wary and excited all at the same time. She found herself wondering whether he looked at every woman that way, and whether it had the same dis-concerting effect on them. Probably.

But even so, tiny goose-bumps still prickled at the back of her neck.

'We thought we'd invite Luca, too,' smiled Lizzy.

Luca rose to his feet, observing the startled look on Eve's face change into one of suspicion. Was she so prickly with all men, he wondered, or just him? He smiled, her frozen face presenting him with a challenge which stimulated him. He threw her a lazy look. 'You didn't mind me gatecrashing your lunch?'

What could she say? That she did? And that wouldn't be entirely truthful, would it? Because her heart was racing with something which felt very close to elation. For here he was, only this time without the hoardes of people there had been last night.

'Of course not,' she said calmly.

Lizzy frowned, as if sensing that something was up and not quite able to work out what it was. 'Um, can I get you both a drink? There's loads of champagne left.'

Eve opened her mouth to ask for something soft and then shut it again. She felt wired up. At a loss. And curiously incomplete. She, who felt at ease in almost any social gathering, suddenly felt an urgent need for something to help her loosen up. 'That would be lovely.'

'Luca?'

'Please.' But he barely heard his hostess speak. He wanted to be alone with Eve, to break down the armoury he had seen her begin to construct from the moment she had walked into the room.

He rose to his feet, with all the grace of some lithe, dark panther and as he moved towards her Eve thought that there was something of the predator in him today. And how did vulnerable animals cope with predators in the wild? They didn't run away, that was for sure. They stood their ground and faced them.

But, dear Lord in heaven—they surely didn't share *her* feelings that this predator—if indeed predator he was—looked good enough to eat.

Like her, he was wearing jeans—faded and washed out and clinging to the hard shaft of his thighs—the pale sweater emphasising the glowing olive skin and the jet-dark eyes. His black hair was ruffled and he was smiling and Eve was aware that, while she had been fiercely attracted to him a decade ago—then she had been teetering on the brink of womanhood with precisely no knowledge of men and their power over women. But now she was experienced enough to know that there were few men of Luca's calibre around.

Achievable goals, she reminded herself and flashed him a bland, pleasant smile.

'So, Eve,' he began. 'Did you make work on time?'

'I did.'

'But you didn't sleep.'

Her eyes widened, for one crazy moment imagining that he had witnessed her fretful night. 'Yes, yes, I did,' she denied automatically.

'Liar,' he murmured as without warning he lifted his hand to lightly touch the delicate skin beneath her eyes. 'This gives you away. Dark shadows, like the blue of an iris, so dark against your pale skin.'

The invasion of her personal space was both unexpected and inappropriate and yet his touch made her tremble, the innocent contact feeling as highly charged as any intimate caress. She wanted to tell him to stop it, to ask him what the hell he thought he was playing at, but she was mesmerised by him, lulled by the deep, honeyed Italian accent. She felt like a weak, tiny kitten, confronted by the blazing strength of a lion. And Italians were tactile, she told herself—that was all.

'I'm not wearing any make-up,' she said, as if that explained everything, bizarrely missing the contact as he moved his hand away.

'I know you're not.' And her scrubbed, pure face intrigued him, too. She must be very assured not to wear any cosmetics, and self-assurance was a potent sexual weapon in itself. 'I didn't sleep myself, if it makes any difference.'

'Should I be interested?'

'Maybe you should, since it was for exactly the same reason as you.'

She pulled herself together. Pretend he's one of those men who plague you, she thought. One of those boring, vacuous men who are attracted to you simply because you're beamed into their homes every morning.

'Lumpy mattress?' she guessed. 'Or simply indigestion after a late night and too much party food?'

He laughed. 'No.'

And then she found herself saying, 'Perhaps there were rather more enjoyable reasons for your lack of sleep.'

'Such as?'

'Oh, I don't know. The blonde woman you were talking to seemed very attentive. Maybe she kept you awake.'

'And does that make you jealous, *tesora*?'

Eve stared at him. Her heart was thumping in her chest. Yes. Yes, it did. 'Don't be so ridiculous.'

He smiled. 'I slept alone.'

'You have my commiserations.'

'Did you?' he drawled.

'Are you in the habit of asking people you don't know their most intimate secrets?'

'I asked you a straight question.' He paused. 'Unlike you, who merely hinted at it.'

'Who you sleep with doesn't interest me in the slightest and I'm certainly not going to tell you *my* bedtime secrets!' she bit back angrily, and wished that she could have disappeared in a puff of smoke as Lizzy chose just that moment to walk back into the room, carrying a bottle of champagne and four glasses.

'Wow!' she exclaimed, her eyes widening like saucers. 'Shall I walk right out and then walk back in again?'

Luca took the bottle from her and began to remove the foil. 'Eve and I were just discovering that we like to get straight to the heart of the matter, weren't we, Eve?'

Eve glared at him, feeling the heat in her cheeks. What could she say? What possible explanation could she give to her friend for the conversation they had been having? None. She couldn't even work it out for herself.

'Well, that's what she does for a living, of course,' giggled Lizzy.

He poured the champagne and handed both women a glass, his eyes lingering with amusement on the furious look Eve was directing at him. 'And what exactly is that?' he questioned idly.

'Go on, guess!' put in Lizzy mischievously.

It gave him the opportunity to imprison her in a mocking look of question. 'Barrister?'

In spite of herself, Eve was flattered. Barrister implied intelligence and eloquence, didn't it? But she hated talking about her job. People were far too interested in it and sometimes she felt that they didn't see her as a person, but what she represented. And television was sexy. Disproportionately prized in a society where the media ruled. Inevitably, it had made her distrust men and their motives, wondering whether their attentions were due to what she did, rather than who she was.

But she wasn't going to play coy, or coquettish, or let Luca Cardelli run through a whole range of options.

'No,' she said bluntly. 'I work in television.'

'Eve's a presenter on *Wake Up!*, every weekday morning from six until nine!' confided Lizzy proudly. 'I've got her on video—would you like to see?'

'Oh, Lizzy, *please*,' begged Eve. 'Don't.'

Luca heard the genuine appeal in her voice and his eyes narrowed. So that would explain why people were watching her at the party last night. Would that explain some of her defences, too? The guarded way she looked at him and the prickly attitude? He shook his head. 'It will be boring for Eve. I'll pass.'

Eve should have been relieved. She hated watching herself, and especially when there was an audience of friends; it made her feel somehow different, when she wanted to be just like everyone else. But, perversely, the fact that Luca *wasn't* interested in watching her niggled her. How contrary was that?

'Well, thank heavens for small mercies.' She sighed, and the sound of the front door slamming and the bouncing footsteps of Kesi were like a blessed reprieve. She put her glass down and turned as a small bundle of energy and a mop of blonde curls shot into the room, straight for Eve, and she scooped the little girl up in her arms and hugged her.

'Arnie Eve!' squealed the little girl.

'Hello, darling. How's my best girl?'

'I hurted my knee.'

'*Did* you?' Eve sat down on the sofa with Kesi on her lap. 'Show me where.'

'Here.' Kesi pointed at a microscopic spot on her

leg as Michael walked into the room, beaming widely.

'Champagne?' he murmured. 'Jolly good. You must come more often, Luca—if Lizzy has taken to opening bubbly at lunch-time!'

'It was only because it was left over from last night!' protested his wife.

'How very flattering,' murmured Luca, and they all laughed.

'I'm *starving*,' said Michael. 'Some of us have been chasing after toddlers in the sea air and working up an appetite!'

'Well, Eve's been up since half-past three,' commented Lizzy.

Luca raised his eyes. 'When you said early, I didn't realise you meant *that* early. Still night-time, in fact.' He looked at her, where only her grey-green eyes were visible over the platinum mop-top of the child. 'Must be restricting, working those kind of hours,' he observed. 'Socially, I mean.'

'Oh, Eve's a career woman,' said Michael. 'She wouldn't worry about a little thing like that!'

Eve twisted one of Kesi's curls around her finger. 'Am I allowed to speak for myself? I hate the term "career woman"—it implies ambition to the exclusion of everything else. As far as I'm concerned—I just do a job which means I have to work antisocial hours.'

'Like a nurse?' interjected Luca, his dark eyes sparking mischief.

'Mmm.' She sparked the mischief right back. 'Or a dairy farmer.'

Their gazes locked and held in what was essentially a private joke, and Eve felt suddenly unsafe.

Shared jokes felt close, too close, but that was just another illusion—and a dangerously seductive one, too.

Lizzy blinked. 'Come and wash your hands before lunch, poppet,' she said to Kesi.

Kesi immediately snuggled closer to Eve.

'Want to stay with Arnie Eve!'

It gave Eve the out she both wanted and needed—anything to give her a momentary reprieve from the effect that Luca was managing to have on her, simply by being in the same room.

'Shall I come, too?' she suggested. 'And we can wash your hurt knee and put a plaster on it—how does that sound?'

Kesi nodded and wound her chubby little arms around Eve's neck and Eve carried her from the room, aware of Luca's eyes watching her and the effect of that making her feel self-conscious in a way she thought she had grown out of long ago.

But when she returned, lunch was set out on the table by one of the windows which overlooked the water, and Luca was chatting to Michael and barely gave her a glance as she carried the child back into the room and, of course, that made her even *more* interested in him!

She settled Kesi into her seat and frowned at Lizzy, who was raising her eyebrows at her in silent question. Just let me get through this lunch and I need never see him again, she thought. And the way to get through it was to treat him just as she would anyone else she was having a one-off lunch with. Chat normally.

But she spent most of the meal talking to Kesi, whom she loved fiercely, almost possessively. Being asked to stand as her godmother had been like a gift, and it was a responsibility which Eve had taken on with great joy.

Lots of women in her field didn't get around to having children and Eve was achingly aware that this might be the case for her. She told herself that with her god-daughter she had all the best bits of a child, without all the ties.

She had just fed Kesi an olive when she reluctantly raised her head to find Luca watching her, and knew that she couldn't use her as an escape route for the entire meal.

'So whereabouts are you living now, Luca?'

He regarded her, a touch of amusement playing around the corners of his mouth. She had barely eaten a thing. And neither had he. And she had been playing with the child in a sweet and enchanting way, almost completely ignoring him, in a way he was not used to.

He wondered if she knew just how attractive it was to see a woman who genuinely liked children. But perhaps he had been guilty of stereotyping—by being surprised at seeing this cool, sophisticated Englishwoman being so openly demonstrative and affectionate. He pushed his plate away. 'I live in Rome—though I also have a little place on the coast.'

'For sailing?'

'When I can. Not too much these days, I'm afraid.'

'Why not? Michael said you were a brilliant sailor.'

He didn't deny it; false modesty was in its way a kind of dishonesty, wasn't it? Sailing had been a passion and an all-consuming one for a while, but passions tended to dominate your life, and inevitably their appeal faded. 'Oh, pressure of work. An inability to commit to it properly. The usual story.'

The words *inability to commit* hovered in the air like a warning. 'What kind of work do you do?'

'Guess,' he murmured.

He had the looks which could have made him a sure-fire hit on celluloid, but he didn't have the self-conscious vanity which usually accompanied an actor. Though he certainly had the ego. And the indefinable air that said he was definitely a leader. 'I'd say you're a successful businessman.'

'Nearly.' He let his eyes rove over her parted lips, wishing he could push the tip of his tongue inside them. 'I'm a banker.'

'Oh.'

'Boring, huh?' he mocked.

She met the piercing black stare with a cool look. 'Not for you, I presume—otherwise you wouldn't do it.'

'Luca!' protested Lizzy. 'Stop selling yourself short!' She leaned across the table towards Eve and gave the champagne-softened, slightly delighted smile of someone who had landed a lunch guest of some consequence. 'Luca isn't your usual kind of banker. He owns the bank!'

Eve felt faint. He *owned a bank*? Which didn't just put him into the league of the rich—it put him spinning way off in the orbit of the super-rich and all the exclusivity which went with that. And there she had been thinking that he might have been impressed with her small-town media status!

She knew he was watching her, wanting to see what her reaction would be. That type of position would be isolating, she realised. People would react differently to him because of it, just as they did with her—only on a much larger scale, of course. On camera she had learned *not* to react, a skill which came in very useful now.

'I didn't realise that individuals *could* own banks,' she said interestedly. 'Isn't that rare?'

He felt as if she was interviewing him! 'It's unusual,' he corrected. 'Not exactly rare.'

'It must be heady stuff—having that amount of power?'

He met her eyes. 'It turns women on, yes.'

She didn't react. 'That wasn't what I meant.'

He ran a finger idly around the rim of his glass. 'It is like everything else—there are good bits and bad bits, exciting bits and boring bits. Life is the same for everyone, essentially—whether you clean the bank or own the bank.'

'Hardly!'

The black eyes gleamed. 'But yes,' he corrected softly. 'We all eat and sleep and play and make love, do we not?'

She willed herself not to blush. Only an Italian could come out and talk about making love at a respectable family lunch! 'That's certainly something to consider,' she mused. 'How long are you staying?'

This was interesting. So what had made her soften? The mention of sex or the fact that he was in a position of power? 'I haven't decided.' His eyes sparked out pure provocation. 'Why? Are you going to offer to show me round?'

'Of course I'm not! You already know the Hamble, don't you?' she reminded him sweetly. 'No, I just thought that maybe you might like to come into the studio one morning—I'm sure our viewers would be interested to hear what life as a bank-owner is like!'

The jet eyes iced over. So she was inviting him onto her show, was she? As if he were some second-rate soap star! 'I don't think so,' he said coldly.

She had offended him when she had only meant to distance herself, and suddenly Eve knew that she had to get out of there. He didn't live here. He owned a bank, for heaven's sake—and he had the irresistibly attractive air of the seasoned seducer about him. Achievable goal, he most definitely was not!

'Pity,' she murmured. 'Well, any time you change your mind, be sure and let me know.' She pushed her chair back. 'Lizzy, Michael—thank you for a delicious lunch. Kesi,—do I get a hug and a kiss?' She enveloped her god-daughter, then took a deep breath. 'I'll say goodbye then, Luca.'

He rose to his feet and caught her hand, raising it slowly to his lips, his eyes capturing hers as he brushed his lips against her fingertips in a very continental kiss.

Eve's heart leapt. It felt like the most romantic gesture she had ever experienced and she wondered if he was mocking her again, with this courtly, almost old-fashioned farewell. But that didn't stop her reacting to it, wishing that she hadn't said she would leave, wishing that she could stay, and…then what?

He's passing through, she reminded herself and took her hand away, hoping that the smile on her face didn't look too regretful.

'Goodbye, everyone,' she said, slightly unsteadily.

CHAPTER THREE

ONCE outside, Eve felt a sense of relief as the cool air hit her heated cheeks. Her pulse was racing and her stomach felt as churned as if she had been riding a roller coaster at the fairground. Though maybe that was because she had only picked at the delicious lunch at Lizzy and Michael's.

But deep down she knew that wasn't true. It was simply a physical reaction to Luca, and in a way it was a great leveller. She wasn't any different from any other woman and she defied any other woman not to react in that way, especially if he had been flirting with you. And he had, she was acutely aware of that. She might not be the most experienced cookie in the tin, but she wasn't completely stupid.

She walked over the rain-slicked cobblestones towards her cottage, listening to the sound of the masts creaking in the wind and thinking how naked they looked without their sails. It wasn't that she didn't meet men—she did—she just rarely, no, *never* met men like that. Which wasn't altogether surprising. Outrageously rich, sexy Italians weren't exactly turning up in the quiet streets of Hamble in their hundreds—or even in the TV studio.

She would go home and do something hard and physical—something to bring her back down to earth and take her mind off him. What did her mother always used to say? That hard work left little room for neurotic thoughts!

She changed into her oldest clothes—paint-spattered old khaki trousers and an ancient, washed-out T-shirt with 'Hello, Sailor!' splashed across the front. Then she put on a pair of pink rubber gloves, filled up a bucket with hot, soapy water and got down on her hands and knees to wash the quarry tiles in the kitchen.

She had just wrung out the cloth for the last time when the doorbell rang, and she frowned.

Unexpected callers weren't her favourite thing. She liked her own space, and her privacy she guarded jealously, but that came with the job. One of the reasons she had never moved away from the tiny village she had grown up in was because here every-one knew her as Eve. True, local television wasn't on the same scale as national—she had never been pestered by the stalkers who sometimes threatened young female presenters—but she was still aware that if your face was on television then people felt a strange sense of ownership. As if they actually *knew* you, when of course they didn't.

She opened the door and her breath dried her mouth to sawdust. For Luca was standing there, sea breeze ruffling the dark hair, his hands dug deep into the pockets of his jeans, stretching the faded fabric over the hard, muscular thighs.

'Luca,' she said. 'This is a surprise.'

'Is it?'

The question threw her. Helplessly she gestured to her paint-spattered clothes, the garish pink gloves, which she hastily peeled from her hands. 'Well, as you can see—obviously I wouldn't have dressed like this if I was expecting someone.'

The black eyes strayed and lingered on the message on her T-shirt and he expelled an instinctive little rush of breath. 'And there was me, thinking that you had worn that especially for me,' he murmured.

'But you don't sail much, any more, do you?' she fired back, even though her breasts were tingling and tightening in response to his leisurely appraisal. 'And strangely enough—the shop was right out of T-shirts bearing the legend: "Hello, Banker!"' She wanted to tell him to stop staring at her like that and she wanted him to carry on doing it for ever.

He laughed, even though he had not been expecting to, but it was only a momentary relief. His body felt taut with tension and he ached in a way which was as surprising as it was unwelcome. He did not want to feel like some inexperienced youth, so aroused by a woman that he could barely walk. And yet, when she had left the lunch party, she had left a great, gaping hole behind.

'Are you going to invite me inside?' he asked softly.

She kept her face composed, only through a sheer effort of will. 'For?'

There was a pause. 'For coffee.'

It was another one of those defining moments in her life. She knew and he knew that coffee was not on top of his agenda, which made her wonder what was. No. That wasn't true. She knew exactly what was on his mind; the flare of heat which darkened his high, aristocratic cheekbones gave it away, just as did the tell-tale glitter of his eyes.

She could say that she was busy. Which was true. That she needed a bath. Which was also true. And then what would he do?

'I need a bath.'

'Right now?' he drawled. 'This very second?'

'Well, obviously not *right* now.'

He looked at her curiously. 'What have you been doing?'

'Scrubbing the kitchen floor,' she answered and felt a sudden flare of triumph to see curiosity change to astonishment.

'Scrubbing the kitchen *floor*?' he echoed incredulously.

'Of course. People do, you know.'

'You don't have a cleaner?'

'A cleaner, yes—but not a full-time servant. And I've always liked hard, physical work—it concentrates the mind beautifully.'

The hard, physical work bit renewed the ache and Luca realised that Eve Peters would be no walkover. He decided to revise his strategy. 'Well, then—will you have dinner with me tonight?'

She opened her mouth to say, Only if I'm in bed by nine, but, in light of the tension which seemed to be shimmering between them, she thought better of it. And why the hell was she automatically going to refuse? Had she let her career become so dominating that it threatened to kill off pleasure completely?

'Dinner is tricky because of the hours I work, I'm afraid, unless it's a very early dinner and, as we've only just finished lunch, I don't imagine we'd be hungry enough for dinner.' She opened the door wider. She was only doing this because he had once been kind to her, she told herself. And then smiled to herself as she thought what an utter waste of time self-delusion was. Why not just admit it? She didn't want him to go.

'So you'd better come in and I'll make you some coffee instead.'

The innocent invitation caught him unawares and something erratic began to happen to his heart-rate even though he was registering—rather incredulously—that she had actually turned down his invitation to dinner.

Her eyes glittered him a warning. 'But I don't have long.'

'Just throw me out when you want to,' he drawled, in the arrogant manner of someone who had never been thrown out of anywhere in their lives.

He closed the door behind him with a certain sense of triumph, though he could never remember having to fight so hard to get a simple cup of coffee. 'These houses were not built for tall men,' he commented wryly as he followed her along a low, dark corridor through into the kitchen.

'That's why a woman of average height lives in it! And people were shorter in those days.'

The kitchen was clean and the room smelt fresh. An old-fashioned dresser was crammed with quirky pieces of coloured china and a jug of copper-coloured chrysanthemums glowed on the scrubbed table. From the French doors he could see the sea—grey and angry today and topped with white foam. 'I love the Hamble,' he said softly.

'Yes, it's gorgeous, isn't it? The view is never the same twice, but then the sea is never constant.' She studied him. 'What's it like, coming back here?'

He stared out at the water, remembering what it had been like when he had first sailed into this sleepy English harbour, young and free, unencumbered by responsibility. It had been a heady feeling.

'It makes you realise how precious time is,' he said slowly. 'How quickly it passes.' And then he shook himself, unwilling to reflect, to let her close to his innermost thoughts. 'This house is…' he searched for just the right description '…sweet.'

Eve smiled. 'Thank you. It's the old coastguard's cottage. I've lived here all my life.'

'It isn't what I was expecting.'

She filled the kettle up. 'And what was that?'

'Something modern. Sleek. Not this.' And today *she* was not what he expected, either. His pulse should not be pounding in this overpowering way. He tried telling himself that he liked his women to be smart and chic, not wearing baggy clothes with spots of paint all over them, and yet all he could think about was her slender body beneath the unflattering trousers, and his crazy fascination for the flirty pink varnish on the toes of her bare feet.

Eve made the coffee in silence, thinking that he seemed to fill the room with his presence and that never, in all her life, had she been so uncomfortably aware of a man. Maybe, subconsciously, she was unable to make the transition from starstruck adolescent to mature and independent woman. Maybe, as far as Luca was concerned, she was stuck in a timewarp, for ever doomed to be the inept waitress with a serious crush. Her heart was thundering so loudly in her ears that she wondered if he could hear it. 'How do you like your coffee?' she asked steadily.

'As it comes.'

But the kettle boiling sounded deafeningly loud, almost as loud as her heart. She turned and looked at him. He was leaning against the counter, perfectly still, just watching her. And something in his eyes made her feel quite dizzy. 'So?' she questioned, in a voice which sounded a million miles away from the usual way she asked questions.

He smiled. 'So why am I here?'

'Well, yes.'

He let his gaze drift over her. 'I couldn't help myself,' he said, with a shrug, as if admitting to a weakness that was alien to him.

Eve stared back at him. She tried telling herself that she wasn't like this with men. She worked with men. Lots of them—some of them gorgeous, too. Yet there was something different about Luca—something powerful and impenetrable which didn't stop him seeming gloriously accessible. Sensuality shimmered off him in almost tangible waves. He was making her feel vulnerable, and she didn't want to be.

She could feel the slow burn of a flirtation which felt too intense, and yet not intense enough. Part of her was regretting ever having asked him into her house, where the walls seemed to be closing in on her, and yet there was some other, wild, unrecognisable part of her that wished that they could dispense with all the social niceties and she could just act completely out of character. Take him upstairs and have him make love to her, just once. That was what he wanted; she knew that.

But life wasn't like that, and neither was she.

'Explain yourself, Luca,' she commanded softly.

There was only one possible way to do that and it wasn't with words. He moved towards her and noticed that she mutely allowed him to, her eyes wide with a mixture of incredulity and excitement. As if she couldn't quite believe what he was about to do.

But she made no move to stop him, and he could not stop himself. He brushed his fingertips over the strong outline of her jaw with the intent preoccupation of someone who was learning by touch.

He felt her shudder, even as he shuddered, and then he caught her in his arms, his breath warming her face, his lips tantalisingly close to hers.

'What do you think you're *doing*?' she gasped.

'I am about to kiss you,' he said silkily. 'Surely you can recognise that, *cara*?'

'You mustn't.'

'Why not?'

'Because…because it's *inappropriate*!' she fielded desperately. 'We hardly know each other!'

'Have you never kissed a man who is nearly a stranger?' he murmured. 'Isn't there something crazy and wonderful about doing that?'

Nearly a stranger. There was something so forbidding about that comment, and she tried to focus her mind on it, but all she could feel was the fierce heat of his body and it was remorselessly driving all rational thought from her head. She pushed her hand ineffectually at his chest. 'That's beside the point, and besides—how do you know I don't have a boyfriend?'

He gave a low laugh. 'You should not have boys in your life, Eve—there should be only men. And there is no one.' He drifted a careless fingertip to trace the outline of her lips. 'Even if there is, he is nothing to you. For you do not want him, *cara*. You want me.'

It was ruthless, almost cruel, but it was true. She did.

He read the invitation in her widened, darkened

eyes and brought his mouth crushing down on hers, and as her own opened in sweet response he felt desire jackknife through him with its piercing, flooding weight.

'Oh,' she sighed helplessly. *'Oh!'*

He smiled against her lips, sensing capitulation, and Eve dissolved, her fingers flying up to his shoulders, her nails biting into his flesh as she felt her knees begin to buckle and threaten to give way. She could taste her breath mingling with his and her body melting against his as he pulled her hard against him.

Vainly, she fought for control, for some kind of sanity. 'Luca, for God's sake—'

He lifted his head and looked down at her, his dark eyes almost black as they burned into her. 'What?' he whispered.

'This is crazy. Mad. I just don't *do* this kind of thing!'

'You just did,' he pointed out arrogantly. 'And you want to do it again.'

Yes, she did. She had given him the bait to play masterful and he had taken it and she liked it. Maybe too much. She wondered if he was masterful in bed and the hard, luminous brilliance in his dark eyes told her that, yes, he probably was. But would he give as well as take?

'You do.' He laughed as he felt her move restlessly against him. 'Oh, yes, you do.'

It was a statement, not a question and she didn't answer, just pressed her hips against his and she felt him jerk into hard life against her, heard the almost tortured little moan he made.

'Signore doce in nel cielo!' he groaned. He couldn't remember the last time it had felt like this.

And although he couldn't work out why it should feel that way—and why with this woman—at that moment he didn't care. Deliberately he circled his hips against her, so that she could feel the rock-hard cradle of him.

The tight band of wanting inside her snapped, exploded into a need so fervent that Eve was swept away by it. She ran her fingers through his hair while he kissed her, his lips moving from mouth to cheek, to neck and back to her mouth again, and she was transported into a whole new land. A place where nothing mattered other than the moment, and the moment was now.

'Luca!'

It was a strangled little cry. A pleading. A prayer. A need which matched his. He had thought that she might try to resist him and he was taken aback by her eagerness. With an effort he dragged his lips from the pure temptation of hers, his breathing ragged, his normal sang-froid briefly deserting him. For this was wild and sweet and instant and unexpected. Like being driven by a terrible aching hunger and stumbling upon a feast.

He captured her face between his hands, his eyes burning into her. 'Your bed?' he demanded. 'Take me there—now.'

Dear Lord! Her blood was on fire—any minute now and she would go up in flames. She felt strength and weakness in equal measures, overwhelmed by a desire which banished everything other than the need to have him close to her, as close as it was possible for a man and woman to be.

But it was not right. It could not possibly be. How did he see her—as one of those women driven only by some kind of carnal hunger? And, more importantly, how would this make her feel about herself?

With an effort she tore herself away from the temptation of his arms. 'No. Stop it. I mean it. I can't.'

He stilled, his eyes narrowing in question, feeling the deep, dark throb of frustration. He steadied his breathing. 'What?' The word came out as hard and clipped as gunfire.

'I shouldn't have done that. I'm sorry, Luca. I got carried away.' His face was like stone, but she guessed she couldn't blame him. She had behaved like the worst kind of woman—she had led him on and left him wanting, and left herself aching into the bargain.

'You certainly did.'

'It's just…hopeless, isn't it?'

He arched her a look of imperious query. 'Hopeless?'

She shrugged her shoulders as if in a silent request that the sudden icy set of his features might melt, but she met no answering response. 'Of course it's hopeless—you live in Rome, I live in England.'

His laugh was sardonic. 'I thought we were going to spend the afternoon in bed,' he drawled. 'I wasn't planning to link up our diaries for all eternity!'

She stared at him. 'How very opportunistic of you!'

'Only a fool doesn't seize opportunity when he is presented with it.'

And only a fool would give him house-room after a statement like that.

'I think you'd better leave, don't you?' she said, in a low voice.

'I think perhaps I had.' The black eyes were lit now, sparking with angry fire. 'But perhaps I could give you a word of advice for the future, *cara*.' He drew a deep, unsteady breath. 'Don't you think it unwise to lead a man on to such a point if you then change your mind so abruptly? Not every man would be as accepting of it as I am.'

She stared at him incredulously. 'What are you saying?' she demanded. 'That I have no right to change my mind? That "no" sometimes means "yes"?'

'That is not what I am saying at all,' he ground out heatedly. 'I mean that a lot of men might have attempted to *persuade* you to change your mind.'

'Well, they wouldn't have succeeded!'

'Oh, really?' The black eyes mocked her, challenged her. 'I think you delude yourself, Eve. I think we both know that if I had continued to kiss you, then your submission would have been inevitable.'

'Submission?' she demanded incredulously. '*Submission?* Tell me, just which century do you think you're living in?' She stared at him furiously. 'Words like that imply some kind of gross inequality. When I make love with a man, I don't *submit*, and neither does he! It's equal. It's soft. It's gentle—'

He gave a short laugh. 'You make it sound like knitting a sweater!'

Her cheeks flamed as she instantly understood the implication behind his words. That it would *not* be soft and gentle with *him*, and her pulses leapt even as she steeled her heart against him. 'Just go. Go. Please.'

'I am going,' he said, in a voice which was coiled like a snake with tension, though not nearly as tense as his aching body. 'But something like this cannot be left unfinished.'

Oh, but it could!

His eyes glittered. 'Goodbye, *cara*,' he said softly.

She watched him go with a terrible yearning regret, standing as motionless as a statue as she heard his footsteps echoing over the flagstones in the hall, her body stiff and tense like a statue's—and when she heard the front door slam behind him she should have felt an overwhelming sense of relief.

So why the hell did she feel like kicking her foot very hard against the wall?

CHAPTER FOUR

ALTHOUGH he wasn't due to fly back until the following morning, Luca changed his ticket and returned to Rome early that evening and remonstrated with himself for the whole two-hour journey. What in the name of God had come over him? What had he been playing at? Coming onto her with all the finesse of some boy just out of high school, acting like some hormonally crazed adolescent.

He stared out of the window, the dull ache in his groin still nagging at him, perplexed by the intensity of need she had aroused in him.

He could have clicked his fingers and had any number of beautiful women and—far more importantly—she was most definitely *not* his type. So why her?

Because she had at first been chilly and offhand with him—studying him calmly with those intelligent grey-green eyes? Because she had answered him back? And then resisted him? Had all these combined to make Eve Peters into a woman he had never before encountered?

Unobtainable.

He was home in time to shower and change, and on impulse he took Chiara out. He hadn't seen her in a long while and she was eager to tell him about her new film. It was late, but she agreed instantly to have dinner with him, and yet her suppressed excitement acted like a cold shower to his senses and he began to regret the invitation the moment he had made it.

Her black hair fell like a sultry night to a waist encased in silver sequins and he thought of Eve in her paint-spattered T-shirt, and glowered at his menu. She flirted outrageously with him all night and laughed at all his jokes and gazed at him as if he were the reason that man had been invented.

The paparazzi were waiting when they left the restaurant and in the darkened light of the taxi Luca narrowed his eyes at her suspiciously.

'Did you tell them where we were eating?' he demanded.

She shook her head. 'No, *caro*—I promise you!'

He didn't believe her. Women said one thing and meant another. They plotted and they schemed to get what they wanted. She tried to drape her arms around his neck. He could smell expensive scent and he found it cloying.

Gently, he pushed her away.

'I will drop you off at your apartment,' he said tersely.

'Oh, *Luca*!' Her voice was sulky. '*Must* you?'

He thought of Eve. Of the melting taste of her lips and the way she had exploded into life in his arms. The cool, composed exterior masking the surprisingly hot and sensual nature which lay beneath, of which he had seen only a tantalising glimpse. He sighed as he stared out at the bright lights of night-time Rome and realised that he must have her.

Should he send flowers? Few women could resist flowers. But then her job probably provided her with plenty of bouquets, so that they would be nothing out of the ordinary.

No, definitely not flowers.

'Goodnight, Chiara,' he said gently.

The car drew to a halt, and the actress flounced out.

'Take me home—and quickly!' he shot out, and the car pulled away again.

Eve tried not to think about Luca at all, though it took a bit of effort.

She never underestimated the cruelly dissecting power of the camera for it picked up on just about everything and then magnified it tenfold. A kilo gained made you look like a candidate for the fat camp and a spot seemed to dominate your face like a planet. And not just the external stuff, either. Doubt and insecurities became glaringly obvious under the lens. If you lost your nerve and your confidence, the audience stopped believing in you and started switching off, and once that happened, you didn't have a job for long.

So she tried to put Luca Cardelli out of her mind by analysing it and putting it into context. It wasn't as if it was anything major, after all. She had simply met a man she had once been mad about, and she was mad about him still. It just happened that he was living in another country, was the wrong kind of man to fall for, and had made a pass at her, clearly expecting her to fall into bed with him at the drop of a hat.

Thank heavens she hadn't.

She decided that she needed to get out more. Meet more people. Spread her wings a little.

She signed up for an afternoon course in French and decided that the next time the crew went out for lunch on Friday, she would join them. And she would take Kesi out for the day on Sunday.

But when she arrived home from work a few days later there was a postcard sitting on the mat, its glossy colour photo providing welcome relief in between all the boring bills and circulars. She liked postcards, though people never seemed to send them much any more—she guessed that was the legacy of travel becoming so much more accessible and unremarkable, and the advent of the email, of course. But there was a magic about postcards which electronic stuff somehow lacked.

She sucked in a sharp, instinctive breath of excitement when she saw where the postcard was from.

Roma.

The photo was unusual and bizarre—it showed a sculpture of two boys and a rather threatening and grotesque animal.

She didn't need to turn it over to know who it was from; she knew only one person who was there. And she didn't need to see his name signed at the bottom to recognise the writing, because somehow she had guessed that he would write like that.

Like a schoolgirl with a crush, she let her gaze drift longingly over his handwriting, like someone discovering a lover's body for the first time. In black ink, it curved sensuously across the card, like a snake.

It said: 'I expect you know the cherished legend that Rome was founded by Romulus—here is a photo of him with his twin brother Remus, suckling on a she-wolf! Any time you're in Rome, then please look me up. It was good to see you. Luca.'

And his phone number.

Eve read it and re-read it, her heart beating fast, feeling ridiculously and excessively pleased while trying to tell herself she shouldn't. It was only a post-card, for heaven's sake! And there was no way she would ever ring him.

But she propped the card against the kitchen window, with the backdrop of the sea behind it, and she looked at it, and smiled, because that simple and civilised communication made her able to put that whole passionate yet unsatisfactory scene out of her mind.

But Luca couldn't get her out of his mind, though he did his level best to—that was when he wasn't incredulously checking his phone messages.

She hadn't rung him!

He shook his head in slight disbelief. Did she not realise the intense honour…? He frowned. No. Honour would be too strong a word, and so would privilege—but he wondered just what Miss Eve Peters would say if she realised that he *never* gave his phone number out to a woman he had only just met!

He stripped off his clothes and stepped into the shower, standing beneath the punishing jets of water with a grim kind of anticipation. Maybe she was playing hard to get. He smiled as he reached for the shampoo. Give her until the end of the week, and she would be bound to ring.

Eve was just setting off for her car when one of the production assistants stopped her. 'Eve—a man rang for you.'

'Did he say who he was?'

The production assistant assumed the expression of someone who had been dieting successfully all week, only to be offered a large cream cake minutes before she was due to be weighed. She was getting married in a month, Eve remembered.

'No.'

'Oh, well—thanks, anyway. If it was important, I expect he'll ring again.'

'He was...' the assistant gulped '...*foreign.*'

Annoyingly, Eve's heart went pat-a-pat, then missed a beat completely. 'Oh?' she said, with just the right amount of studied casualness.

'Italian, I think,' the assistant continued. 'He sounded absolutely *gorgeous*! All deep and accented and sexy. You know what they say about a come-to-bed voice? Well, he must have been the man who invented it! Who *is* he?'

'I have absolutely no idea,' replied Eve airily, feeling a brief pang of sympathy for the girl's fiancé. 'And it irritates the hell out of me, when someone doesn't bother to leave their name!'

Which wasn't quite true. What was irritating the hell out of her was her irrational response to the fact that it had undoubtedly been Luca. What was he doing, ringing her? Ringing her at work, too!

And would he ring again? At home? Until she reminded herself that he didn't have her number. But she was in no doubt that someone like Luca could always get hold of a woman's number...

It had been many years since Eve had made excuses to hang around the house, hoping that someone might call her, and she hated it almost as much as she couldn't seem to stop herself from doing it. Every time the phone rang she jumped like a startled rabbit, but it was never him.

Finally, frustrated with herself—and with *him*, though she wasn't quite sure why—she went round to see Kesi and ended up staying for afternoon tea. And it was predictably typical that when she arrived home the red light on her answering machine was winking at her provocatively.

With trembling fingers, she clicked the button and his deep, dark, rich Italian voice began to speak. Just like him, she thought as she listened. Deep and dark and rich.

'Eve? I find that business brings me to London next week. How would you like to meet for dinner?' A tinge of amusement entered the voice. 'An early dinner, of course—leaving you plenty of time to get home for your allotted hours of sleep. Ring me.'

She was appalled to find herself replaying it four times, while silently wondering whether or not to return his call, even while, deep down, she knew with unerring certainty that she would be unable to resist.

But she left it for three days, even though the self-restraint it took nearly killed her. And when she finally got round to it, she had to field her way past a very aloof-sounding secretary who, once she had switched from Italian to perfect, seamless English, sounded very doubtful as to whether Signor Cardelli would wish to be disturbed.

Clearly Signor Cardelli would.

'Luca?' said Eve tentatively, wishing that she could rewind the time clock and never have dialled the wretched number.

Luca felt his body instinctively tense. So the *strega* had made him wait, had she? He couldn't remember ever having had to wait for anything in his life.

'Eve?'

'Yes, it's me! I got your message.'

'Good.' He waited. Now let her see how it felt.

Eve clutched the telephone tightly. Damn him! 'About dinner.'

'Mmm.'

She felt like slamming the phone down, and realised that might be overacting by just a tad. Did she want to have dinner with him, or not? Well, yes and no.

Luca's eyes narrowed. Did she always make it this difficult for men? And then he remembered the way she had been in his arms. They had been so close to going up to her bedroom, and... The tension increased. 'Would you like to have dinner with me, Eve?' he questioned silkily.

Yet another defining moment. Her life seemed to be full of them, and Luca Cardelli always seemed to have something to do with them. Eve swallowed. Pretend you're live on camera. Give him a briskly pleasant, take-it-or-leave-it attitude. It would be so much easier if she *could* just leave it, if the thought of not seeing him again didn't seem as if her world would then take on a rather dull and monochrome appearance.

'That would be lovely. When?'

She was making it sound as though she had been invited to tea with a maiden aunt!

'I arrive on Friday evening,' he said coolly. 'So how about Saturday?'

She supposed that she could pretend to be busy— but what would be the point in playing games if the outcome would only make her miserable?

'Saturday sounds good,' she said evenly, but her heart had started racing.

'Excellent. I'll ring you when I'm in England. *Ciao, bella.*'

Eve found herself staring at the handset, to realise that he had hung up. Her mouth had dried with pure excitement, which quickly changed into another emotion she didn't quite recognise and wasn't up to analysing because there was only one thought dominating her mind right then.

Dinner on Saturday. An early dinner so that she could get back in plenty of time for the early night necessary for her early start.

But she didn't work on Sundays. She knew that and he knew that.

Sunday was her lie-in day.

CHAPTER FIVE

THE hotel was one of those modern, quietly expensive places which often seemed to be featured in glossy magazines and were a million miles away from the featureless anonymity of the large chains.

Eve walked into a foyer painted a deep, dark navy with shiny wood floors and expensive-looking rugs. She had to look hard for the reception desk, which was clearly designed not to *look* like a reception desk. It was half hidden by vases of clashing scarlet and violet flowers and the sleek blonde who eventually gave her a smile looked as if she should be modelling in a glossy magazine herself.

She guessed that this was one of those exclusive places, so hip and cool that it was almost icy, and she shivered at the thought of what she was about to do. Although, as she reminded herself fiercely—she didn't have to do anything. Not if she didn't want to.

'Can I help you?' said the blonde.

'Um…' Oh, for heaven's *sake*—when did she last preface a question with the word, 'um'? 'I'm meeting Mr Luca Cardelli here at six.'

The blonde's cool face didn't flicker. '*Signor* Cardelli,' she corrected, 'should be here—'

'Any minute now,' came the honeyed tumble of his words and Eve's mouth dried as she turned round to see him emerging from the lift. 'Hello, Eve.'

He looked, she thought rather desperately, utterly

ravishing—in a dark linen suit, and a blue silk shirt which was unbuttoned at the neck, showing a tantalising glimpse of olive skin and the arrowing of dark hair.

'Luca,' she said, her voice very low. She forced a smile. 'Hello.'

He narrowed his eyes. This was not the behaviour of a woman who wanted him to make love to her. In fact, she looked as though she were dancing on pieces of broken glass. Did that mean she was nervous, and if so—wasn't that rather endearing? At least it showed him a chink in her sophisticated armour.

He smiled and moved forward, kissing her on each cheek, his hands on her shoulders, continental style, and Eve felt herself relax slightly. Anyone would think she was a timid little mouse of a thing, with no experience of men whatsoever!

But as she breathed in some subtle, heavenly aftershave he was wearing, and felt the faint rasp of his chin against her cheek, it struck her that she felt completely naïve and inexperienced. Why, give her a plate of prawns and she would probably drop them all over him!

'You look wonderful,' he murmured. More than wonderful—though distinctly understated. Some floaty little silk skirt and a soft, pink sweater, which moulded itself to her perfect breasts. A pair of high suede boots and her hair caught in a plait and tied at the end with a pink ribbon. It was both sexy and yet wholesome and it had the effect of making him want her even more.

'Thank you.'

'Shall we go and eat?' He glanced briefly at his watch. 'What time do you have to leave?'

'Oh, well, I can decide later,' she prevaricated. She met the look of curiosity in his eyes. 'That is—um, there's a train at nine-thirty.' Which wasn't answering his question at all, and she had said 'um' *again*!

'We could eat here, if you like. Or find somewhere local?'

Oh, heavens. Normally sure and decisive, she suddenly felt a quivering mass of uncertainty, until something happened which made her get real. Maybe it was the fleeting side-glance which the sleek blonde at Reception sent her, as if she would give anything to be in Eve's shoes.

Enjoy this, she told herself. Just enjoy it. 'What's the food like here?'

'I have no idea.' He glanced around. 'My secretary booked it for me—it's a little—antiseptic for my taste. But there's a sushi bar around the corner—do you like sushi?'

'I love it.'

'Come on, then.'

Outside, the whirr of traffic and the people walking made Eve feel more relaxed, and the sushi bar was gorgeous.

'I think this restaurant might have been designed by a feng shui expert,' she commented as they were shown to a low table, next to a blurred and restful painting.

'Because you have to be a contortionist to sit down?'

She smiled. 'Don't you think it has a rather restful air about it?'

Restful?

He thought that he could have been given some long sleeping draught and he still would have felt the constant heat of desire, but maybe that was because he had been on a knife-edge of delightful anticipation and uncertainty all week. And uncertainty could be a heady emotion—as if you had discovered some new and delicious food you had not realised existed.

Like a natural predator finding itself in undiscovered terrain, he narrowed his eyes and handed her the menu as the waitress hovered.

'Shall we order?'

They discussed the menu together, but Eve might as well have been selecting sawdust and treacle for all the notice she took of the food which began to arrive, on stark, square plates, pretty as individual pictures. She did her level best to eat it, determined to act as normally as if she were out with any attractive man, and not one who seemed to have the power to reduce her to a kind of melting jelly with just one hard, brief smile and one glitter of those brilliant, yet unfathomable dark eyes.

She sipped her wine and felt about seventeen, and just hoped to goodness that the face she presented was calm and serene.

Luca leaned back in his seat. 'So tell me how you came to be a television star.'

'*Presenter,*' she corrected immediately and caught his look of mocking question and smiled. 'I know I'm a bit defensive, but the job comes with so much baggage that it's almost instinctive.'

'People wanting to know you for the wrong reasons?' he guessed.

'Something like that.' She sipped at her wine. 'I expect you've been a victim of it yourself.'

'Never a victim, *cara*,' he murmured. 'And it is not a word I would have associated with you. So tell me about it.'

She loved the way he curled his tongue around the word *'cara'* and found herself, bizarrely, wishing that he would speak to her in Italian, even though she barely knew more than a few words of the language. 'I did a degree in meteorology at university. The weather had always fascinated me, but when you grow up in a place where so much is determined by it, it seemed kind of natural. Then the local station was looking for a weathergirl, and I applied for the job, without really thinking I'd get it.'

'Because?'

'Oh, because I wasn't blonde and busty—and most of the other candidates were!'

'Yet they chose you,' he observed softly.

'Yes, they did—it seemed that they weren't looking for a pneumatic blonde, but someone who actually knew what they were talking about, and the viewers seemed to like me. Then the regular presenter left to have a baby, and the next thing I knew they were asking me to fill in for her—temporarily, at first. But they asked me to stay on, and I did, and that was nearly three years ago, which is actually quite a long time in television.'

'And you like it?'

She hesitated. 'Yes, I do—though sometimes it doesn't really seem a serious job, something that matters, like being a brain surgeon. But I'm aware that I'm lucky to have it—and realistic to know that it won't last for ever. Television jobs rarely do.'

'And when it ends?'

She met his eyes, and shrugged. 'Who knows?'

'So you have no other ambitions, other than what you do now?'

Eve twisted the stem of her glass between her fingers, wary of how much to tell him. But why be a closed book? What would be the point? 'Oh, well, one day I hope to have children, of course.'

He nodded, noting the 'of course', but also her omission of the normal progression of falling in love with a man and marrying him first, but he knew that women were shy of talking of such things, for fear that men would think them needy.

Eve felt exposed. She had done all the talking, and he very little. 'What about you? Did you set out to become the owner of a bank?'

'I don't think anyone does that.' He shrugged. 'I set out to become successful, and somehow it never seemed successful enough. There was always a new challenge, a new obstacle to be overcome and, once I had overcome it, something else to move on to.'

'So now you own a bank, does that mean you've stopped moving on?'

'Oh, no. There's always something else to achieve.'

He stopped speaking abruptly and something about the suddenly wary look in his eyes told her that he had already said more than he was comfortable with.

'I see,' she said slowly, but she thought how restless and nomadic it made him sound. It should have had the effect of distancing her but she found that she wanted to reach her fingertips out and play them along the silken surface of his skin.

He could feel the tension surrounding them as palpably as if it had been a third person sitting with them at the table. Would she play games with him tonight? he wondered.

'Shall I get the bill?'

Something about the way he was looking at her was making her heart pound so loudly that it was as if an entire percussion section had taken up residence in her head. Mutely, she nodded, excusing herself to make her way to the bathroom where she splashed cold water on her wrists, as if hoping that the icy temperature might dull the fevered glitter of her eyes, but to no avail.

They walked out into the darkened street and he turned to her as her hair gleamed like liquid gold beneath the street-lamp. 'Do you want to catch that train?'

She heard a taxi pass them, and she thought of this passing her by. She looked up at him, aware of what hinged on her answer. She looked up into his face and in that moment her heart turned over. 'No.'

He smiled as he bent his head and kissed her in the street. He told himself that he would not have done the same in Rome, where curious eyes would have registered that Luca Cardelli was behaving in a way which would have distorted the image of his cool persona for ever. But that here in London, it was anonymous. And yet it was more than that. She had captivated him, with her cool, intelligent eyes, the way she had made him wait. For a man used to having whatever he wanted whenever he wanted it, it had proved a powerful aphrodisiac. And he could not wait any longer to kiss her again.

'Eve,' he groaned against her moist, sweet lips.

She threaded her fingers into his thick, dark hair as his lips worked a kind of magic, allowing him to pull her closer into his body until she began to tremble uncontrollably, almost relieved when he pulled away, his eyes as black as the night.

'Come,' he said shortly.

He took her hand and they walked in expectant silence back to the hotel, where she saw the receptionist staring at them, and as the lift doors closed on them it occurred to her that it must have been pretty obvious where they were going and what they were doing.

But who cared?

She was a free agent, and so was he. And she wanted him so much that she could barely think, let alone speak, but words were unnecessary because as soon as the lift doors had closed he took her in his arms again, kissing her with an unrestrained passion which took her breath away.

She barely registered the room, except to note that it was heady with the fragrance of flowers and softly lit for seduction. She felt a momentary qualm, half wanting to tell him that this felt slightly out of her league, but wouldn't that just sound like a woman wanting to safeguard her reputation?

But then he began to stroke her, murmuring softly in Italian, threatening to send her already heightened senses spinning out of control, and all her doubts and fears dissolved. Pulling away from him, she met the distracted question in his eyes, and she stroked the hard jaw, as if to silently reassure him. Did he think she was going to change her mind?

'What is it?' he demanded.

'Luca, I don't…I don't have anything.'

He frowned. 'What are you talking about? What don't you have?'

This was worse than one of those sex education books they forced you to read at school, graphic and matter-of-fact, but it was precisely because she *had* read them that she found herself blushing, which seemed slightly ridiculous in the circumstances.

'Contraception. I'm not on the pill. I'm not prepared.'

He gave a slow, sensual smile, her statement appealing to his undeniable machismo. So she was not on the pill—which meant that she did not do this freely with others, and that pleased him more than it had any right to please him.

'Aren't you?' he murmured silkily and moved his hand beneath her skirt, roving it up between her stockinged thighs. He slipped the panel of her panties aside and heard her gasp of pleasure as he pushed a finger into her moist, warm heat. He smiled when she moaned out a protest as he took the finger away and, slowly and deliberately, sucked on it, his eyes capturing hers in a look of erotic promise.

'On the contrary, *cara*,' he whispered, 'it occurs to me that you are very well prepared indeed. And you taste absolutely delicious.'

'Luca!' Her voice trembled briefly and she closed her eyes, feeling strangely shy at his blatant and unashamed enjoyment.

'And fortunately, I am, as you say—prepared.'

Her eyes flew open again to see that he had produced a pack of condoms from his pocket and, while the logical side of her was glad that he had thought of protection, some unrealistic, romantic side of her wished that he hadn't. For didn't that make it somehow *clinical*? Or did he always have them with him, just in case? And even if he did, would that be so bad? Wasn't it better to be careful, and didn't some of her more liberated girlfriends actually carry them around in their handbags?

He saw the brief, vulnerable look which crumpled her mouth and bent his lips to it, teasing it with tiny kisses until it had softened again.

'Stop frowning,' he whispered.

'Make me.'

'With pleasure. But first I want to see your body.'

He pulled the pink sweater over her head and sucked in a raw breath of pleasure as he saw what lay beneath. A sheer bra, sprigged with roses, and the pink-dark tips of her nipples looked as though they were a continuation of the flowers themselves.

'Beautiful,' he murmured. 'Beautiful. Do you always wear such exquisite lingerie? Did you wear it for me, Eve?'

She felt a feline glow of pleasure. 'But of course.' She tiptoed her fingers beneath his shirt and luxuriously began to trickle her fingers over the silken flesh, to alight on one small, hard nipple and to circle it.

He closed his eyes. 'That's good.'

His appreciation gave her the encouragement to begin to unbutton his shirt. She might not have done this for a long time, but she wasn't a complete novice and she sighed with pleasure as, bit by bit, she bared his chest, then peeled his shirt off and dropped it on the floor. Then she dipped her head and gently bit on his nipple, and he groaned before shaking his head. He wanted her naked, and quickly.

Yet he had never felt quite so preoccupied while

undressing a woman, revelling in the sensation of laying her bare. He skimmed off the skirt, the stockings and the panties and then, finally, untied the pink ribbon which bound her hair in the plait.

'Like unwrapping a birthday present,' he said as the hair spilled down over her shoulders, all over her tiny breasts.

She kissed a nipple and felt him shudder. 'When's your birthday?'

'August,' he said distractedly as he kicked off his shoes and swiftly divested himself of the rest of his clothes.

August was months away, and fleetingly she found herself wondering whether they would still be lovers then, but at that moment he lay down on the bed and pulled her on top of him and their warm flesh mingled as he began to kiss her and Eve stopped thinking completely.

He touched her and kissed her with expert lips and fingers, which soon had her making tiny little yelps of disbelief that something could feel so good. But he did it with a certain sense of wonder, too, as if she were the first woman he had ever made love to, and fleetingly she found herself thinking that he had seduction honed to a fine and flattering art.

His eyes were glittering with hot, black fire as he moved above her and she felt strangely and inexplicably shy when at last he entered her with one long, silken thrust.

He wrapped a strand of her hair possessively around his finger as he felt her tighten around him. 'Is that good?'

'It's…' But then he moved and the words were forgotten, her nails digging into his shoulders and her legs wrapping themselves sinuously around his back, pleased when he gave a low moan of pleasure.

'And that?'

'Yes!'

He moved inside her until she felt that she would die with the sheer pleasure of it, and when finally the slow stealth of pleasure exploded into unstoppable fulfillment she was taken aback by the sheer, devastating power of it. Her body continued to tremble as she felt him shudder helplessly in her arms.

They lay there for a while, sweat-sheened bodies locked in the trembling aftermath, until eventually he raised his dark head, kissed the tip of her nose and looked down at her, a rueful smile touching his mouth.

'Well?' he sighed.

She met his eyes. 'Well?'

He laughed, and while the rich, warm sound made her feel safe, it also made her aware of her own insecurities. But that was what happened, wasn't it? She didn't know his sense of humour, or his favourite colour or even where he lived. You met a man and you began an affair with him, and there was always uncertainty about what the future would bring.

He kissed her, his body beginning to ache again and, instinctively, he moved once more, but Eve stilled him with a cautious finger to his lips. 'Be careful.'

He understood immediately and slowly withdrew from her, and the regretful little sigh he made at leaving her made Eve lie back against the pillows, a contented smile of satisfaction on her face. She pillowed her head on her hands and her hair spilled over her like syrup.

'Let me use the bathroom,' he groaned as his eyes lingered on her rose and white nakedness. 'Stay right there.'

Wild horses couldn't have dragged her away. She wasn't going anywhere, she could never imagine wanting to leave until she had to and she wasn't even going to think about it. Dreamily, she gazed up at the high ceiling until Luca came back into the room and joined her on the bed.

'You,' he murmured, kissing her shoulder, 'are amazing. Beautiful.'

She pulled him fiercely against her, and he entered her quickly, but the love he made to her was long and slow and indescribably sweet, and when it was over she snuggled against him, fighting sleep.

He shook her gently. 'Don't you have to catch a train?'

'No.'

'Oh, I see,' he murmured. 'So the train was your escape route, was it, Eve?'

'Mmm.' But now she had no desire to break free. She rested her head against his chest, but he reached over to lift his watch from the locker and gave her a brief smile.

'Forgive me, *cara.*' He yawned. 'I must make one very, very quick phone call. Don't go away.'

But the phone call brought her crashing back down to earth as she lay there and listened while he spoke in rapid Italian. God knew what he was saying or whom he was speaking to. It was only a little thing, but maybe it helped her not to start dreaming impossible dreams.

Luca had another life in another country and she was only a tiny part of it, and who knew for how long?

Maybe for no longer than the morning.

CHAPTER SIX

EVE opened her eyes and in the split-second moment between waking and sleeping she found herself wondering where she was. She saw the rooftops of a London skyline through the uncurtained window, and a man asleep on the bed beside her, and felt the warm laziness which bore testimony to a night of rapturous love-making.

Quietly, she turned her head to look at him. He was truly beautiful in sleep, the deep, regular breaths making his hair-roughened chest rise and fall. He was lying on his side, one hand cupping his face, the long lashes making two ebony arcs which contrasted against the olive-gold of his skin. He looked innocent and indolent.

Turning back to study the ceiling again, she let out a tiny sigh, satisfaction mingling with regret that the night was over.

She hadn't been in this situation for a long, long time, and in fact she had never been in this particular situation, having shed all inhibitions and taken as a lover a man who was, to quote Luca's own words, 'nearly a stranger'.

In fact, she hadn't been in a relationship for almost... She frowned, shocked to realise that it was almost two years. And that had been so different. A slow build-up to a romance that she had known from the beginning would end yet with this one she had absolutely no idea what her feelings were.

It was out of character for her—the cool, calm and considered Eve Peters—to have fallen into bed simply because she found him irresistible. But it must happen to him all the time, she thought.

'So why the frown, *cara*? I thought I had kissed that goodbye, last night.'

She started. She had been so deep in thought that she hadn't realised he was awake. The dark eyes were watchful and shuttered by the lashes, his long-limbed body as still as a tiger lying in the full heat of the sun. Outwardly, so relaxed, but with all that pent-up strength and power lurking just beneath the surface.

She affected a careless smile. 'Was I?'

'Mmm.' Idly, he reached out and began to run his fingers through the rich satin of her hair. It had been an incredible night, but he had known it would be. He had been so hungry for her that it couldn't have been anything else, but now with morning came a desire that was transmuted into a different feeling altogether, as inevitably as night followed day. Then it had been the excitement of the unknown and the undiscovered, the delicious anticipation of waiting to see if she would be his.

And now?

Now he was left with the familiar, and, no matter how wonderful it had been, there was a certain protocol to be followed. There were unspoken rules and he wondered if she understood them as well as he did. Rules about boundaries and expectations. He would not be owned. He had never been owned.

'Come over here and kiss me,' he murmured.

But Eve had seen something in his eyes which had made the tiny hairs on the back of her neck prickle in apprehension. There was something very controlled about him this morning, no matter that she could see for herself the evidence that he wanted her very badly. Physically, in any case. But emotionally? Wasn't there a cool kind of distance in the black eyes which were studying her as one would a horse that had not yet been broken? Waiting to see what she would do next, how she would react.

Was he frightened that she was going to come on all heavy? Afraid that she would become clingy or needy or demanding or any of the other things which women sometimes instinctively did when a man had possessed and pleasured them? Well, he need not worry!

She curved her mouth into a smile, so grateful then to the job which had allowed her to make a living out of hiding what was going on inside. Why, even after the death of her mother, she had been back in the studio within the month, her heart breaking inside and yet able to keep a calm and controlled exterior.

True, a couple of the regular and more perceptive viewers had written in to ask if she was okay, and on the editor's advice she had mentioned the death. Which had led to a whole programme on bereavement, after she'd been flooded with letters from people who had gone through exactly the same thing and were anxious to share their experience and the strength which had grown from it. Television taught you lots about controlling your emotions; very early on she had discovered that the camera *could* lie.

'Why don't you come here and kiss me instead?' she suggested.

He rolled towards her, a lazy smile on his lips. So she was not one who would festoon him with kisses and tell him that he was the most marvelous lover she had ever had?

He lowered his mouth onto hers. 'Like that?'

The sweet, aching beauty of that kiss threatened to take her breath away. Eve closed her eyes.

'Exactly like that,' she whispered huskily.

He made love to her for a long time, seeming to go out of his way to demonstrate his finesse as a lover, and twice she sobbed his name out loud. It had never been like this with a man. Never. But that was the kind of thing you should never admit to—especially to a man with an ego the size of Luca's.

He relaxed as he noted her smile of dreamy contentment, smoothing a few stray strands of hair away from her damp forehead. 'How long can you stay?'

'I'll go after lunch. When's your flight back?'

'At five.' He very nearly offered to change it, but he smiled as he touched his lips to hers. It was a very clever woman who made no demands on a man—someone ought to tell them that that was what kept interest alive!

She didn't leave until three and for the whole train journey home Eve was on a high. Her cheeks were rosy and flushed, her eyes bright and her hair very slightly mussed and she bore all the signs of a woman who had been very thoroughly made love to.

He was gorgeous. Utterly, utterly gorgeous, but she hadn't been stupid enough to go all gooey-eyed on him. She recognised that he was that hard, rare breed of man who was essentially a loner, living life on his terms and his terms alone—and why shouldn't he? Wasn't that exactly how she lived her own life?

And as long as she remembered that, there was no

reason why they couldn't have a wonderful and mutually fulfilling love affair.

The green fields rumbled by and she closed her eyes, recalling the lazy morning they had had, not getting out of bed until just after noon, and then strolling to a nearby pub for lunch, where Luca had been engaging and amusing company.

It would be all too easy to fall for him, hook, line and sinker, and she knew instinctively that she must be on her guard against losing her heart to him. She would play it slow and careful. He had told her that he would ring, and she would be very patient and wait.

Well, no—that wasn't *quite* true. She wasn't going to *wait*—for what use was a life spent waiting as if that were the only thing which mattered? She would live her normal life, she reasoned. She would be happy and fulfilled, and look forward to his phone call when it came.

Her state of euphoria lasted for precisely three days, by which time he hadn't rung and Eve fell into the age-old trap of feeling insecure and stupid.

Why had she launched straight into a love affair with him, when she had known nothing of his expectations of it, nor been given a chance to express her own? Though, how could she have done? Wouldn't it have been the kiss of death to have quizzed him about what he wanted, or tell him what she wanted—especially when she didn't know?

Why couldn't she take it for what it was, and simply enjoy it? And maybe she could have done. If only he would phone.

It was nearly a week before she heard from him and when she picked up the receiver and heard his drawled and sexy Italian accent, her instinct was to slam it right down again or demand to know why he had taken so long, though she suppressed it.

Instinct could be a very dangerous thing.

And besides, hadn't just the sound of his voice sent her heart racing into overdrive?

'Eve?'

'Hello, Luca.'

So cool, he thought admiringly. She had been on his mind a lot. She knew his number, both at home and at the office and he had given her his mobile— but she had not contacted him, nor sent him a text message, which women invariably did.

In a way it had been a kind of test to see if she needed him, and now that she had proved she did not, he wanted to see her.

'How are you?'

'Oh, you know. Busy. What about you?'

'I've been to Amalfi.'

'That's on the coast, isn't it?'

'Indeed it is. It's where I keep my boat.'

'And is it very beautiful?'

'What, the boat or the coast?'

Eve laughed. Damn him! Laughter could be just *so-o-o* seductive! 'Both.'

'Both are indeed *very* beautiful, just like you.' He paused. 'I've missed you.'

Not so much you couldn't pick the phone up, she thought, but the remark pleased her. 'Good,' she answered evenly. 'It's always nice to be missed.'

'And have you missed me, too?'

'Stop fishing for compliments!'

He laughed. 'So when am I going to see you?'

'That depends.'

'On what?'

'On whether we have corresponding free dates in our diaries.'

Even cooler! 'You mean you wouldn't cancel something if it meant seeing your Italian lover?' he murmured.

Oh, the arrogance! 'Certainly not,' said Eve. 'Would you?'

Curiously enough, he thought about jettisoning his proposed trip to the States, but for no more than a moment.

'Probably not,' he agreed, and then paused. 'So when?'

'Suggest some dates and I'll see if I'm free.'

'I have to go to New York next weekend—how about the weekend after that?'

'Okay,' she agreed. 'Where? In London?'

'Why don't you fly out to Rome?' he suggested casually.

Eve had never been to Rome before, and a city was never more beautiful than when you saw it through the eyes of someone who actually lived there. Luca on his home territory.

His penthouse apartment was on the Viale Trinita dei Monti, close to the Spanish Steps and it was to-die-for. Minimalist and modern—all stainless steel and frosted glass. The floors were mahogany and there was Carrara marble in the bathrooms. The rooms were almost all white, but the lights could be adjusted to create different colours and moods and the floor-to-ceiling windows showed the most amazing views over the city.

Outside was a terrace with tall terracotta pots with lemon trees growing and smaller ones with rosemary, sage and lavender plants—so that the warm air was scented with their fragrance.

It was, thought Eve as she stood and looked at Rome, the apartment of a man with no ties, nor room for any.

He showed her colonnades and palaces and churches until she was dizzy with the splendour of it all and so he drove her out of the city to the picturesque town of Tivoli, perched on a steep slope amid pretty woods and streams.

'This is just so beautiful,' she murmured as she gazed across at the twisted silvery olive trees of the Sabine Hills.

He touched her hair. 'So are you,' he said softly, and took her back to his apartment, where he spent the rest of the afternoon making long, slow love to her.

That evening, in a restaurant off one of the narrow, cobbled streets of Trastevere, they ate the simple, delicious *tonnarelli cacio e pepe* by candlelight, and drank wine as rich as garnets.

They lingered over coffee and Eve felt utterly relaxed. 'Tell me about your childhood,' she said lazily. 'Where were you born?'

'I am a Roman,' he said simply. 'I was born here.'

'And you never wanted to live anywhere else?'

He gave her a slightly mystified look and a very Latin shrug of his shoulders. 'Why should I? Everything I want is here.'

It gave her an insight into his fierce love for his country, his city.

'And your family? Where are they?'

'My sister lives in Rome also. My parents are both dead.'

Eve dropped a lump of sugar into her espresso. 'Mine are, too,' she said, though she noticed he hadn't asked.

'Then we have much in common,' he murmured, and his eyes glittered a sensual message all of their own. 'Apart from the very obvious.'

It was a blatant, sexual boast and she supposed it should have pleased her, but oddly enough it made her feel insecure. Because surely sexual attraction was a very ephemeral thing?

'Come, Eve.' He signed the bill which the waiter had placed in front of him, and looked at her. 'I think it is time to go home now, don't you?'

But once they were back in the apartment, Luca rubbed a finger at the tiny crease between her brows. 'Frowning, always frowning—ever since we left the restaurant! You know what happens when you frown?' he teased. 'Lines appear and there they stay, and no woman likes lines on her face.'

For some reason, the remark rankled. 'And when lines do appear, then we magic them away with surgery, isn't that right?' she questioned acidly. 'For while lines on a man's face denote experience—on a woman's they damn her with age!'

'*Cara, cara*—that is your judgment, not mine. You work in an industry which is defined by age.' He kissed the tip of her nose. 'And I am certainly not advocating the use of surgery!'

She thought that he wouldn't have to. She turned to look out over the glittering lights of the city. Men like Luca prized beauty, and wasn't youth synonymous with beauty? He would always have his pick of young, firm and unlined flesh.

'Eve?'

His voice was deep and low and beguiling and she closed her eyes as he began to rub his fingertips over her shoulders, pulling her back into the hard, lean contours of his body. Why spoil this? she thought as his hands moved round to cup her breasts? 'Mmm?'

'You are angry now? Fiery?'

She laughed and turned to him, smoothing her hand down over the chiselled outline of his jaw. 'Not angry, no, but fiery, yes.' Her eyes glittered him a teasing provocation. 'Always fiery.'

'Then come here and show me,' he breathed as he saw her mouth curve in a look of hunger. 'Show me.'

'Oh, I'll show you all right,' she said unsteadily as she began to unbutton his shirt.

That night she played the dominant role, undressing him and teasing him until he groaned for mercy. She kept her stockings on and straddled him as her hair flailed about her shoulders and she thought that she had never felt quite so uninhibited with a man.

And afterwards he lay there in silence for a little while, before eventually opening his eyes and giving her a rueful look.

'Wow,' he breathed.

She felt flushed and brimming over with confidence and with life. 'You liked that?'

He gave a lazy smile. Caught a lock of her hair and pulled her head down so that their lips were a whisper apart. 'Oh, sì, cara. I liked it. I liked the way you were so wild and so free.' He slipped his hand between her legs and she gasped. 'And you like that?' he murmured.

She began to squirm with pleasure. 'Oh, God— yes. Yes! Please don't stop.'

The smile became a growl of a laugh, like a lion.

'Stop? Let me tell you, *cara mia*, that I haven't even started yet.'

But the weekend came to an end all too quickly and at the airport he kissed her with a passionate goodbye which left her reeling.

'Stay an extra day,' he murmured into her ear.

The temptation almost overwhelmed her. Reluctantly, she withdrew a body which felt as though it could quite happily stay glued to his for ever.

'I can't,' she said regretfully. 'I have an early studio call in the morning.'

He nodded, dropped a kiss on the top of her head. 'I am away in the States for a month,' he said. 'And I will call you. Very soon.'

'Do.' She squeezed his hand and walked away, clutching her overnight bag.

Was that the irony of life? he wondered as he watched her sashaying towards the departure lounge with just a careless wave and a smile as she disappeared. That you always wanted what you couldn't have? If she had been living in the same city, there was no way he would have asked her to stay an extra day! Protectively, he would have wanted and guarded his own space.

He turned and began to walk away, oblivious to the women who watched him as his mobile phone began to ring and he slid it from his pocket and began to speak.

Eve arrived home in time to run herself a bath before bedtime, which she enjoyed by candlelight, dreamily and rather sentimentally listening to some Italian opera as she soaked in the lavender-scented suds.

And she was as bright as a button the next morning, despite a weekend of very little sleep, handling a sulky teenage pop star with aplomb and cleverly questioning the local Member of Parliament about why so little was being done about local traffic congestion.

In fact, she was on cloud nine, not really living in the real world but existing instead in the perfect world of the imagination, where life was like that weekend all the time. Until she reminded herself that life was never that good. It couldn't be, could it? Because it wasn't real.

Maybe it was because when you took a lover, he dominated your normal routine and drove everything else into the shadows. Especially when it was someone like Luca.

Was that because he lived so far away, and therefore the bits of him she got were the exciting, glamorous bits, with none of the everyday drudge bits in between, which usually made you view a relationship much more realistically?

If he were living up the road in the same village and they had settled into a grinding routine, then would she still feel this crazy floating-on-air feeling?

It was a couple of weeks later that she happened to glance up at the calendar on the kitchen and her eyes stayed fixed on it with a mounting sense of disbelief, her heart missing a beat of very real fear.

She was late.

Very late.

She carried on preparing her stir-fry, even though her hands were trembling, but when the fragrant rice and prawns were served out on a pretty plate decorated with sunflowers, she pushed it away, her appetite gone.

She was never late. Never, ever, ever. Not once in her life—why, she could have set her clock by it. Was that why she hadn't noticed it before, because she took it so much for granted? Or was it because her thoughts and her senses had been so full of Luca?

But she couldn't be pregnant. They had used condoms and they had been careful.

She tried to ignore it, but couldn't, clicking onto the search engine of her computer, to discover that there was a three percent chance the contraception could have failed. She felt sick, until she told herself that the odds were still hugely in her favour.

For a while longer she allowed herself to hope, but it was a hope which became increasingly forlorn.

The days became a series of long, agonised minutes while she waited and waited for something to happen which stubbornly refused to happen.

Luca rang and she tried to chat normally, but inside her head was screaming with the terrible reality of her situation. They hadn't even made a definite arrangement of when to meet, but where last week that would have bothered her, this week it barely even registered.

Seeing Luca was the furthest thing from her mind. She just wanted the confirmation that this was nothing but a hiccup, a bad and scary dream and that she wasn't pregnant.

But she was an intelligent woman who could not hide from the truth, however unpalatable. Fearful of discovery and wagging tongues, she drove out of the village to the nearest large, anonymous chemist to buy herself a pregnancy kit, and by the end of the day uncertainty became fact.

She stared at herself in the mirror as if expecting to see some outward sign that she had changed, but there was nothing. Her cheeks were still tinged with roses, her eyes bright and shining. Perhaps a little *too* bright and shining.

Didn't they always say that pregnant women looked the picture of health?

And that was her. Healthy and yet terrified out of her tiny mind, because she was pregnant with Luca Cardelli's baby.

CHAPTER SEVEN

Eve tugged at the crisply clean duvet cover with a little more vigour than was necessary and then looked round at her bedroom, checking the room like a chambermaid. Luca was coming to stay and she had felt honour-bound to go through the motions of welcoming him.

Clean linen, fresh flowers and scented candles waiting to be lit. Would it resemble some kind of over-the-top boudoir?

She sank down onto the bed and promptly creased the cover. She didn't care. In fact, she didn't care about anything. How could she, when she was privy to a piece of news which was about to change the whole course of her life?

Listlessly, she glanced at her watch. Luca would be here within the hour and she had better get her act together. She was going to have to tell him, she decided, and sooner rather than later. And besides, she doubted whether she would be able to keep it secret from him. How could she look into his eyes and pretend that nothing had changed?

It was such a big secret that it seemed to have taken over her life—she had half expected people at work to stop her in the corridor and congratulate her, because she felt so obviously pregnant.

But if people *did* know—then they were hardly going to congratulate her, were they? A woman who found herself unexpectedly pregnant, without a steady, loving partner, tended to find herself an object of sympathy—even in these enlightened times. Oh, women made the best of it, and there was no reason why she shouldn't make her life—and the life of her child—a wonderful, glittering success. But there was no doubt that at the beginning, at least, it wasn't exactly news to send champagne corks flying.

How the hell was she going to tell Luca? Should she blurt it out straight away, or wait for the 'right' moment? And if such a moment existed, it would soon disappear, for she could predict what his reaction would be.

He was going to be furious. What man wouldn't? To find that they were going to become a father to the child of a woman who was 'nearly a stranger'?

She heard the sound of a car approaching, of a door slamming and murmured words carried on the wind. Through the antique lace of her bedroom curtain, she saw the tall, dark figure as he paid the taxi driver.

He was here. She should have been excited but her heart felt numb, with fear and dread the only emotions she was capable of feeling.

Luca glanced up at the cottage, his eyes narrowing. Had that been Eve up there, watching him? And if so, why hadn't she pulled back the curtain and waved?

His mouth hardened. You met a woman you thought was sexy and intelligent and uncomplicated and suddenly she started playing the diva. She had sounded strained on the telephone, the way a woman sounded if you forgot her birthday. Was she sulking already? And if so, why?

He lifted his hand and banged on the brass knocker. He was here now. He thought of her slender, tight body, the way she had ridden him to heaven and back, and felt the corresponding throb of desire. Who cared if she was sulking? He would kiss away her pique and make her sigh with pleasure for two whole days. And after that?

Almost imperceptibly, he shrugged.

The door opened and Eve fixed her brightest smile onto her face. 'Luca!' And flung her arms around him, mainly so that her eyes would give nothing away. Not yet. Not yet.

He smiled against her hair and dropped his bag to the floor. Better. Much better. 'Have you missed me, then, *cara mia*?'

Act as you usually would, she told herself as she drew her head away, a small smile playing at the corners of her mouth. '*Missed* you? I'm a very busy woman, Luca Cardelli—I don't have time to miss anyone!'

It was what he would have once deemed a textbook answer. A woman who did not make him centre of her universe. A woman with a life of her own. Perfect. But oddly, it did not please him. He *wanted* her to tell him that she had missed him. Break through her cool patina of sophistication. To conquer her, he realised, with a grim kind of shock. He liked to conquer his women. And once he had conquered them, he moved on.

'Come in. What would you like to do first? I could make us some tea and then we could go for a stroll down by the sea—' But her words were blotted out by his kiss, the seeking splendour of his lips, and she froze, like a block of ice in his arms.

Not yet. She couldn't. Not yet.

'Luca!' She pulled away. 'Anyone would think that you had come here with only one thing in mind,' she teased remonstratingly, her heart pounding, still with that terrible constricting fear.

'You don't want to take me straight upstairs and make love?' he demanded. 'You want *tea*?'

'Well, don't you? You've been travelling all day! Come on, I'll put the kettle on!' As she marched towards the kitchen she was acutely aware that she was coming over like a cross between a domestic drudge and a schoolmarm.

He followed her into the kitchen, his eyes narrowed with irritation. What kind of a greeting was this? Did she think that he had flown all the way here to be marched into her kitchen like a hungry schoolboy?

'You know, an Italian woman would never treat her lover so,' he observed, on a sultry note of caution.

Slowly, Eve turned around. 'Then I suggest you find yourself an Italian lover, instead of an English one.'

'Tell me, do you give all your men such a careless greeting?'

His silky question made it sound as though she had a line of lovers stretching as far back as the eye could see! Eve felt sick and the sickness reminded her of the secret—such a tiny secret at the moment—which was growing inside her belly.

And suddenly she realised that her instinct had been correct all along and that there wasn't any such thing as a 'right time' to tell him. To wait would be to perpetuate the deception and to let him make love to her first would be unthinkable. And much too poignant. Tell him when he was naked and she was vulnerable? She couldn't.

'Sit down, Luca,' she said heavily.

Luca's eyes narrowed. Something did not add up. He had been given an inkling that something was not right from the moment he had arrived, but he had put it down to nerves, even though there had been no nerves during that deliciously enjoyable weekend in Rome. She wasn't the kind of woman to be shy at showing him her home—for a start, he had already seen some of it and she wasn't insecure enough to need *his* approval about where she lived.

So what was it?

Silently, he pulled out a chair and sat down, stretching out his long legs, his expression poker-faced and shuttered.

Eve's nerve suddenly failed her. 'I'll just finish making the tea,' she blustered

Still he watched and waited.

Eve tipped boiling water in the teapot, making a drink that she knew neither of them would touch, but it seemed important to be going through the motions of doing *something*. And why didn't he *say* something? Why was he just sitting there, like a brooding dark and golden statue? Why wasn't he asking her what was wrong and then she could have blurted it out, instead of having to say it cold, searching for words to cushion it and knowing deep down that there were none.

'I'm pregnant.'

For a long, tense moment, Luca thought that he was dreaming, or in the middle of a nightmare.

'Turn around and look at me,' he said softly. 'And say that again.'

Her hands gripping onto the sink as if for support, Eve sucked in a hot, painful breath and turned around to face him. She had expected to see anger, fury, disbelief, but there was none of these things. His eyes were as cold and as forbidding as black ice and his face was like that of a stranger. She looked at him and felt as though she hardly knew him, and she didn't, she supposed, not really.

And yet, even now his child was growing inside her.

'I'm pregnant.'

His eyes roved to her belly, looking for a tell-tale swell, but the sweater she wore told him nothing.

He nodded. 'That is why you didn't want to make love.'

Something in the calmness of his voice washed over her like a balm and for the first time since she'd found out she felt a small degree of comfort. He was an intelligent and perceptive man—he had obviously realised that no earthly use would be gained from anger.

'That's right. I just felt that it would be *inappropriate* in the circumstances.'

He gave a low, contemptuous laugh. 'Inappropriate? For whom? For you, or for your baby—or for the poor fool who fathered it?'

She had thought that anger could only be expressed in a loud and furious storm, but Eve realised at that moment that there was another, different kind of anger. A quiet and scornful kind of anger which was far more deadly. She stared at him, her eyes full of consternation, not quite understanding—for if blame could be apportioned, then it was equal blame, surely? If fault was to be found, then they were both at fault.

'Luca—'

His icy words cut across her as if she hadn't spoken. 'Were you already pregnant the night you slept with me?' he hissed. 'Or was there just a chance that you might be?' He gave a low, bitter laugh, barely able to believe that he had been so sucked in by her offhand attitude that he had pursued her like a schoolboy!

His black eyes bored into her like daggers. 'Won't this complicate things for you?' he questioned sardonically. 'I should not think that the father will offer support if he finds out that you have been intimate with another!' Another low, bitter laugh. 'Well, do not worry, *cara*. He will not hear it from me! I will take it to the grave with me.'

His eyes were cold, she thought. So cold.

'And I hope to God that I never set eyes on you again as long as I live,' he finished woundingly.

As if she were a spectator watching a play, Eve watched him get up from the chair, her lips parting in disbelief. It was as if she were watching him in slow motion and something had taken away her powers of speech, for he was almost at the door when she managed to bite the words out.

'But you…you're the father, Luca!'

This time the silence seemed to go on for ever. He felt rooted to the spot, as if he had just been turned to ice, yet the blood which roared around his veins was as hot as the fires of hell.

'What?'

It was a single word, shot out like a threat, as if

daring her to repeat her statement again, but she had to. She *had* to.

'You're the father.'

He turned round and laughed. 'I am not the father!'

And something in his arrogance and contempt brought the real Eve back to life. The real, strong Eve, though a very different woman now. She had to be, nature had decreed it. How dared he? She thought of the life within her, created by accident and now denied by its biological father, and a slow fury began to simmer inside her.

She held her head up proudly. 'I can assure you that you are.'

His heart pounded. 'Prove it.'

Now it was her turn to look at him witheringly. 'I have no intention of ''proving'' it. And besides, I don't need proof, Luca—I know.'

'How?'

'Because I haven't slept with another man for two years!'

'You expect me to believe this?'

'I expect *nothing*!' she retorted. 'I am telling you simply because I believe it is your right to know—though, God knows, I wish I hadn't bothered now!'

He was nodding his head, as if a blindingly simple solution had just appeared before him. 'Of course,' he said. 'Of course.'

Eve sucked in a deep breath. Calm down, she told herself. It isn't good for you and it isn't good for the baby. He was bound to be shocked at first and go off at the deep end—who wouldn't after a momentous piece of news like that? She looked at him hopefully. 'Of course, what?'

He nodded once more. 'I understand perfectly now.'
'You do?'

'Sure. It's all coming back to me. That night in London, when you told me you wanted children. I remember you saying it, it struck me at the time. And you're a career woman, aren't you, Eve? A woman with a high profile and a demanding job. So who needs a man around? A baby is what you wanted, isn't it? A designer baby—women do it all the time, these days. And who better to father your baby than one of the richest men in Italy? Well, clever, clever, *cara*.'

He stared at her as if she were a particularly unappealing creature who had just landed from outer space. 'But I'm interested to know how you did it. Perhaps you deliberately scratched your pretty pink fingernails through the condom when you were putting it on? If so, it was an ingenious plan.'

She felt as though he had slapped her. 'Get out,' she said. 'Get out of here before I call the police and have you thrown out!'

But he didn't move. 'How much do you want?' he asked insultingly. 'A one-off payment, is that what you had planned?' He looked around at her pretty, cottagey kitchen and his lips curved into a disdainful smile. 'I expect you earn pretty good money, don't you, Eve? But my kind of wealth is way out of your league. With my money you can afford all the things you really want—the best nanny, a bigger house, a fancy car, holidays. Isn't that right, *cara*?'

'Don't *ever* call me that again!' she spat out. 'I'm giving you one last chance to leave, Luca, and if you don't, then God help me, but I *will* call the police!'

He glanced at the clenched fists by her sides. His temper was on such a knife-edge that he knew he had to get away. For all their sakes. And the fact was the she carried his child, and, though the method she had used was unforgivable, that fact remained.

'I am leaving,' he said coldly.

'And don't come back! I never want to see you again!'

He plucked a wallet from his jacket pocket, and for one awful moment Eve thought that he was going to throw some money down in front of her. But instead he extracted an expensive-looking business card and placed it on the table with calm and steady fingers.

'That's the address of my lawyer,' he said carefully. 'I'll let him know that you'll be in contact.'

And with those damning and insulting words ringing in her ears, Eve listened in disbelief as his footsteps echoed down the corridor and the front door slammed shut behind him.

This was getting to be something of a habit, she thought tiredly. But once he had gone, she felt oddly lighter—as though a great weight had been lifted from her shoulders, and until it had gone she hadn't realised just how much she had been dreading telling Luca.

His reaction had been even worse than her worst imaginings, but at least now it was over. The obstacle had been faced and overcome. Whatever happened now, nothing could be as bad as that had been, surely.

And then she remembered the cold anger on his beautiful face and she bit her lip, tears threatening to well up in her eyes, but she swallowed them down.

There was no point in thinking about it, or him. It was over.

She heard a protesting rumble in her stomach, and for the first time since she had found out the news, she felt hungry.

You've got a baby to feed, Eve Peters, she told herself sternly as she opened the fridge door.

CHAPTER EIGHT

'THERE has been no phone call?'

The lawyer shook his head. 'Nothing, *signore*.'

'And you telephoned her, as I instructed?'

'I have attempted to telephone Signorina Peters on four occasions, and on each occasion she has steadfastly refused to take my call.'

Beneath his breath, Luca swore. He turned to the window, his mind turning over the facts in his cool, clear-headed way.

But for once, he was perplexed.

This had been the last thing he had expected. Her words of protest he had naturally assumed to be false, her declaration that she never wished to see him again he had thought was the defiant words of a woman who meant no such thing but was simply playing a clever game. He hadn't been sure what it was she had wanted—him or his money, or both— but he had been certain that he would find out soon enough.

But indeed it seemed that she *had* severed all contact.

He continued to stare unseeing as the midday sun illuminated the magnificent spectacle of Roman rooftops, and then his heart clenched in fear.

Unless…unless there was a very good reason why she *hadn't* contacted him. Inside the pockets of his trousers, his fingers clenched themselves into tight fists.

What if...what if there was no longer any reason for her to do so? What if the pregnancy no longer existed?

For a moment Luca felt physically sick, and, for a man who had rarely known a day's sickness in his life, it was an unwelcome sensation. But then, he was getting quite used to those.

'Signor Cardelli?'

Luca turned around, surprising the look of concern on the face of his lawyer.

'You are sick, *signore*?'

Resolve returned to fill his blood with the fire of determination and Luca shook his head. 'No, my friend. Not sick at all,' he said grimly. It was time to take matters into his own hands. Something that he should have done weeks ago.

Eve cheerily said goodbye to the crew, but once she was headed for her car and her driver her smile faded. It was hard work trying to pretend that nothing was wrong, and she didn't know how much longer she would be able to keep it up.

Sooner or later she was going to have to tell Clare, her editor, and it had better be sooner rather than later, before she, or someone else on the show, guessed her secret. And it wouldn't take a member of the regional crime squad to do that.

Twice this morning she had had to leave the set, trying not to rush out to the bathroom, where she had been violently sick. She had stood before the mirror, trembling, before rubbing some blusher into her cheeks and hoping she looked halfway decent. She wasn't going to be much use as a breakfast presenter if she spent all her time throwing up.

But even if, as the doctor had suggested, the sickness passed—and, infuriatingly, by the end of the show all the nausea *had* passed—the fact remained that she was soon going to become very obviously pregnant.

No. She was going to have to make an appointment to speak to Clare.

She walked out into the bracing air, glad of the welcoming coolness after the stifling atmosphere of the studio, and as she looked around for her car her heart missed a beat.

For there, leaning against an unfamiliar silver car, stood a figure, as still and as all-seeing as if he had been hewn from a deep, dark marble. He was dressed all in black, and it made his hair and eyes look like the night. For one wild and crazy moment she thought about running inside, like a woman seeking refuge from the storm, but she knew that she could not.

She had to face him.

He studied her almost obsessively, searching for signs. Any signs. But the thick, sheepskin coat she wore enveloped her like a big, warm cloud and all he could see was her pale face and the green-grey eyes which glittered so warily at him.

He began to walk towards her.

'Hello, Eve.'

'I don't want to talk to you.' Desperately, she looked around the car park, deserted save for the swish silver car he had been standing beside. Where the hell was her driver? He was *never* late.

'I think we need to talk,' he said steadily. Last time he had been caught off guard in all kinds of ways. He had flown off the handle and raged in a manner which was guaranteed to achieve nothing. And Luca had always been an achiever.

She turned to him, unprepared for the effect he had on her. The way her heart crashed against her ribcage. The way her legs felt weak. She should feel nothing but contempt for him, the same as he so obviously did for her—so why wasn't it that easy? Why did she still feel outrageously attracted to him? But that was purely physical, she reminded herself. And she was more than just a physical person. Much more.

'I don't think you understand, Luca,' she said quietly. 'In a minute my driver will be here and I will get in the car and go home. Without you.'

'I am afraid that is where you are wrong.'

She stared at him uncomprehendingly.

'Your driver has gone. I sent him away.'

'You *sent him away*?' she repeated disbelievingly.

He pointed to the long, low silver machine. 'I have a car and I will take you anywhere you want to go, but I need to talk to you and I *will* talk to you. You owe me that.'

She hugged her coat tighter around her. 'I owe you nothing after the despicable things you accused me of.'

Again, he nodded, sucking in a deep, dry breath. 'I had no right to make those accusations, but I was…'

Her eyes were curious. 'What?'

He sighed. 'I felt as though my whole world had been detonated.'

'So the thought of fatherhood didn't appeal?' she said flippantly, because that seemed the only sure-fire way to hide her hurt. She shrugged. 'Then there's nothing left to say, really, is there?'

He froze. 'Are you telling me that there is no baby?'

It took a moment for the meaning of his words to dawn on her and, when they did, it was once again like being hit by a hammer-blow. Did he think…did he really think…?

'God, Luca,' she gasped, as if he really had struck her. 'Could your opinion of me get any lower?'

'What am I supposed to think?' he demanded heatedly. 'When you refused to take my calls!'

'Your lawyer's calls,' she corrected him. 'Because I didn't want to do *business*, that's why I didn't take them.'

'So?'

'Yes, there is still a baby,' she said slowly. 'But don't worry your head about it—it's *my* baby and it won't have anything to do with you.'

He could see her teeth beginning to chatter. 'Get in the car,' he said.

'No.'

'Please.'

The voice was deceptively soft and Eve felt so weak from the flurry of emotions he had provoked and simply from the impact of seeing him again that she could not have possibly refused. 'Oh, damn you,' she said indistinctly, but she did not walk away.

He opened the passenger door, but she shook off his arm as he attempted to guide her into the seat.

'I am *not* an invalid! Just pregnant!' And then, terrified that someone from the crew might be lurking around, she cast her eyes around anxiously, but there was no one except for them, and she expelled a sigh of relief.

He noted her reaction and it told him a great deal. So no one knew; of that he was certain. She had kept the pregnancy hidden. Why?

He started the engine. 'Where do you want to go?'

'Home.' She leaned her head back against the rest and closed her eyes, daring him to talk to her, to accuse her and harangue her, but to her surprise he didn't. The warmth and movement of the car lulled her, reminding her of just how tired she was. But tiredness came in great strong and powerful waves these days.

He glanced over at her, watching as her breathing became deeper and steadier. She was asleep. Around the steering wheel of the car, his leather-covered hands relaxed a little.

The sheepskin coat had fallen open, and her thighs were indolently apart and relaxed in sleep and he felt an unexpected and unwelcome shaft of arousal. Damn her! he thought. Damn her and her unstudied sensuality. He fixed his eyes on the road ahead.

The car drew to a halt and Eve snapped her eyes open, momentarily disorientated. She was outside her cottage, with Luca in the driving seat beside her.

She fumbled for the handle. 'Thank you for the lift.'

'I'm coming in.'

'No, you're—' But she heard the note of determination in his voice and knew that she was fighting a losing battle. And besides, had she really thought that he would come all this way, drop her off and then just go off again with a little wave goodbye? She would hear what he had to say, and then he could go.

The cottage felt cold. Stiffly, Eve took her coat off and didn't protest when he took it from her fingers and hung it up in the hall. She shivered. 'I'm going to light a fire.'

'Let me do it.'

She raised her eyebrows. 'Do you know how?'

He actually laughed. 'Of course I do. There are many things you do not know about me, *cara*.'

'I'm going to make some tea,' she said. Anything to get away from his presence, which, in the small, dim hall, seemed to overwhelm her.

When she returned with the tray he had managed to produce a roaring blaze. She put the tray down on a small table and watched him. 'I wouldn't have thought there would be much cause for fire-making in your fancy apartment.'

'No,' he agreed as he threw a final log on. 'But we had a place out in the country where we used to holiday when I was a little boy. Very basic. That's where I learned.'

It was odd to think of this assured, arrogant man as a little boy. Would she have a boy, she wondered, and, if she did, would he look like Luca? A beautifully handsome little boy, a permanent reminder of passion and its folly.

He moved from the fire to the tea-tray and poured them both a cup, and while part of her felt slightly resentful that he had walked into her house and now seemed to be taking over, the other part was so tired that she was glad to let him.

But it was dangerous to be passive. He had told her quite clearly what he thought of her and she could not and should not forget that. 'You'd better say what it is that you want to say, and then go—I'm very tired.'

Yes, he could see that for himself. Beneath her fine grey-green eyes were the blue-dark traces of shadows.

'Are you sleeping?'

'In fits and starts. And, of course, I have to get up very early.'

His mouth thinned. She should have handed her notice in immediately! 'You didn't contact my lawyer,' he observed slowly.

'Did you really expect me to?'

What would she say if he told her yes, of course he had expected her to. A lifetime of experience had made him cynical. His vast wealth had set him apart from the moment he had attained it. And that he would have considered it perfectly normal for her to have attempted to make a huge claim on his fortune. She, above all others, was surely entitled to?

'Yes,' he said simply. 'I did.'

'Well, rest assured—I didn't and I don't intend to. Your money is safe. Was there anything else?'

She was being so cold, so distant, as if ice were running through her veins instead of blood. And could that be good for the baby?

'I want you to have everything you need, Eve.'

'But I do! I have a house and I have a job, a good job.'

He remembered the way she had looked around her, as if worried her words would be overheard. He was pretty certain that her pregnancy was still a secret and his killer instinct moved in; he couldn't help himself. 'But for how long?'

She stared at him. 'Excuse me?'

'Have you told them you're pregnant?'

'That's none of your business.'

'I think it is.' A spark spat in the grate with all the force of a gunshot. 'You may not be employable as a pregnant woman.'

She gave a little laugh. 'There are laws governing that kind of discrimination,' she returned. 'So please don't worry on my account.'

This was going neither the way that Luca wanted, nor had expected. He had expected a little…what? Gratitude? That the past few weeks might have given her time to calm down and see sense. Surely she must realise that his money could make all the difference to her life as a mother?

'I do not want you to struggle for money—not when I have enough, more than enough.'

'But it isn't going to *be* a struggle. I'll manage—'

'I don't want you to *manage*, I want you to be comfortable!'

'What you want is not really what counts, Luca! It is what I say that does!'

'But it is my baby, too,' he pointed out.

'Oh?' She feigned surprise. 'So you're no longer disputing paternity? What happened? Did you have someone run a DNA test on me, while I was asleep?'

'Eve!' Proud, stubborn woman! 'Let me help you,' he said suddenly.

She was still hurting from the things he had said; it was hard to imagine a time when she would not. 'You think your money can buy you anything, don't you?'

His black eyes glittered. 'Would you deny me my child, then, Eve?' he questioned simply.

And something in the way he said it cut through all her defences.

Up until that very moment she had been able to think of the baby almost as an abstract concept—as if it hadn't been real and, even if it had been, it was nothing now to do with Luca. But she was fast discovering that she had been very naïve. By telling him she had involved him, and someone like Luca wouldn't take that involvement lightly.

Oh, why hadn't she kept it secret? He had never intended theirs to be anything other than a short-term love affair. He wasn't the kind of man who would ever settle down, he just wasn't. The affair would have burnt out after a few heady weeks, or months— he would have moved on to the next conquest, the way that men like this always did.

But could she honestly have kept it secret from him? Wasn't it his right to know that his seed had borne fruit? She bit her lip at the irony of it. Because he had never meant it to.

'What do you want?' she asked cautiously.

'I don't know,' he said, and it was the first time in all his charmed and powerful life that he had ever made such an admission. He sat down on the sofa and studied her, the dark eyes narrowed in question. 'You haven't even told me how far advanced you are.'

'Nearly five months.'

Five months! 'Already?' he asked, slightly unsteadily.

'Yes, my bump's hardly showing yet.' She met his eyes, and despaired, for their inky allure still touched a part of her she had decided had to be out of bounds. If he had stayed away—even for a bit longer—she might have become immune to him. But she wasn't—and that didn't help matters. 'Time flies when you're having fun,' she said sarcastically.

Had it really been that long? She must have got pregnant the very first time—before Rome, before he had gone to the States. He remembered with a sinking heart the way he had been incautious, the way he had wanted to make love to her straight after the first time. And she had stopped him.

He frowned. How had so much time passed, almost unnoticed? He had thrown himself into his work since she had first told him—perhaps, he recognised now, using it as a kind of denial therapy. And all the time he had been waiting for the financial demands he was certain would come his way. He had set her a test, he recognised, just as he had right at the beginning when he had waited for her to contact him. And wasn't that what he always did, in his professional as well as his personal life—set impossibly high standards and wait for people to fail to meet them?

Only Eve had not failed.

'Anyway.' She forced herself to be businesslike, because surely that was what it all boiled down to. 'If it's just the finance thing you're worried about, then don't, because I will be fine.' She gave him a bright smile. 'Unless there was anything else?'

He stared at her incredulously. 'You think this is simply about *money*? You expect me to walk out of that door without a backward glance and have no interest in this child of mine?'

This child of mine. Powerful words. Daunting words. But then Luca was a powerful and daunting man.

'I have no expectations whatsoever. I never did have,' she added deliberately and at least he had the decency to flinch. 'You'd better tell me what yours are. Some kind of contact, I suppose?'

'Contact!' he repeated furiously. 'What an ugly word that is!'

'Well, it may be ugly, but it happens to be the relevant word!' she retorted, stung. 'All in all it's a pretty ugly business, isn't it?'

He rose to his feet then, came over to where she sat and crouched down beside her. If it had been any other woman, in any other situation, he would have taken her in his arms, to comfort her and to soothe her. But her frozen stance told him not to try.

All his life, Luca had been able to seduce any woman he wanted, to persuade her round to his way of thinking, but now he suddenly recognised that Eve was not so malleable.

His eyes travelled to the perfect fingernails, painted a coral-pink today, and he remembered his outrageous accusation.

'So what is it to be?' continued Eve remorselessly. 'Every other weekend, with some of the holidays? Alternate Christmases? That's how it works, isn't it?'

'I don't give a damn how it works!' He reached out and caught her face in the palm of his hand and tipped it up to look at him, and to his surprise she didn't stop him. 'There is only one sensible choice which lies ahead of us,' he said, and his perfect English suddenly became a little more broken. And in a way, maybe this was how it was supposed to be. All his life he had run from commitment, but he could run no longer. 'You will marry me, Eve,' he said fiercely.

She looked at him. 'Marry you?' she said incredulously.

CHAPTER NINE

'AND those are the facts,' finished Luca, with a shrug.

'Wow!' said his sister softly, and handed him the sleeping baby.

Luca raised his eyebrows sardonically as his hands tightened automatically around the warm little bundle. 'What's this?' he questioned drily. 'Aversion therapy?'

'Nonsense! You are brilliant with your nephew—you always have been. You're a natural with babies, Luca.'

The baby stirred and sighed and Luca glanced down at him, his hard, handsome features softening. 'Just that it seems I won't get much practice with my own.'

'Oh, Luca—for heaven's sake! It isn't like you to be such a defeatist!'

'I am not being defeatist, Sophia!' he snapped, but the baby made a squeak of protest, so he lowered his voice. 'I am merely being practical. She lives in England and I live in Rome—and we are not together. The facts speak for themselves.'

'Well, why don't you *be* together?' demanded his sister. 'For heaven's sake, Luca, you can't spend your whole life as a commitment-phobe, searching for the impossibly perfect woman. You'll just have to marry her—I can't think of a better reason for breaking your long-term bachelorhood than a baby! People do it all the time!'

Thoughtfully, Luca stroked a tender finger across the glossy raven hair of his nephew and then looked up at his older sister, with an expression in his eyes he could see surprised her.

'I have asked her to marry me,' he said.

'You *did*?'

He nodded.

'And?'

'And she said no.'

There was a moment of shocked, stunned silence, and then, to his astonishment, his sister tipped her head back and burst out laughing, causing her son to squirm in Luca's arms and he handed him back, a stern look on his face.

'I see no cause for laughing,' he said icily.

Sophia wiped the corner of her eyes. 'You don't? Well, I think it's priceless! A woman has turned the great Luca Cardelli down! Do you know, I think I like this woman!'

'It is *not* funny!'

'No,' she said slowly. 'No, I suppose it's not. Well, you're going to have to do something, Luca.'

'I know I am,' he said grimly.

The red studio light went off and there was a burst of spontaneous clapping and Eve looked round and smiled as she saw the executive producer walking into the studio, a sheaf of papers in his hand.

'It went well?'

'Eve, it was absolutely *brilliant*!' He waved the papers like a winner's medal. 'I have here the viewer figures, my dear, and I can say, without fear of contradiction, that we have a hit on our hands.'

She knew they did. It was indefinable, that feeling, but she had worked in television long enough to know success when she encountered it. She had been pretty optimistic from day one, but you never really knew for sure, not until the figures came in.

'We've had a sack-load of letters and emails, the phone hasn't stopped ringing all week and the duty log is full of praise.'

It had all worked out perfectly, so perfectly that she sometimes felt she ought to pinch herself.

She hadn't even had to tell Clare about her pregnancy—the editor had guessed it for herself, and so it seemed had most of the crew. Leaving the set regularly in order to be sick had kind of given the game away.

Her early-morning sickness had shown no sign of abating. And that was when the idea had come up for Eve to be taken off the breakfast show and given her own daily slot just before midday. As someone had remarked, it wasn't exactly a loss to the world of television if they used the show to replace the endless reruns of a comedy which had been made two decades earlier.

Eve In The Morning! was to be modelled on the classic audience-participation theme, but with an added twist. As well as the usual studio discussions on the lines of: 'Too Fat To Enjoy Sex!' or 'My Husband Doesn't Know I'm A Stripper!', there was to be a special five-minute slot every week which would keep the viewers up to date with her pregnancy. Viewers liked to be involved, and what better way to involve them?

'That's fantastic.' Eve smiled broadly at the executive producer, some of the tension leaving her, and she placed her hand over her swollen belly as the baby gave a kick as if to say, Concentrate on *me*, now! Time to go home for a well-earned rest. She picked up her handbag, switched on her phone and it began ringing immediately.

Number unknown.

'Hello?'

'Eve?' The voice was so frosty that Eve was surprised it didn't freeze her slim little mobile phone.

The baby kicked again. It's your daddy, she thought to herself and her initial feeling was one of relief. She had not heard a single word from him since the day she had refused his offer of marriage, which had left her wondering whether Luca Cardelli had washed his hands of his baby. But it seemed he had not.

'Hello, Luca,' she said steadily, and licked her suddenly dry lips. 'Er, I can't really talk now.'

'Why not?'

'Because I'm in the studio and there are a lot of people around—'

'Then find somewhere where there are not!'

There was some note of implacable determination which made her do just that, and she quickly walked out until she found an empty dressing room.

'How are you?' she asked.

He ignored that, drawing in a deep breath in order to keep his temper in check. 'More importantly, *cara*,' he said silkily, 'how are *you* and, more importantly, how is my baby?'

Inexplicably, his possessive statement didn't ruffle her one little bit. Indeed, there was a mad, stabbing maternal pride that he chose to acknowledge his child like that. She sighed. Sometimes you just couldn't argue with nature.

'I'm fine. Well, I am now. They took me off the breakfast show because I was being so sick—and they've given me my own show—'

'I know they have,' he interrupted coldly.

'You do?' Eve frowned in confusion. 'But we don't transmit to Italy!' she said, rather stupidly.

'I am not in Italy.'

'Then wh-where are you?' she asked, but even as she asked it she knew what the answer would be.

'I'm in the Hamble.'

A nameless dread crept over her. 'What are you doing there?'

'We'll discuss that later,' he clipped out. 'I think we'd better meet for lunch, don't you, Eve?'

It was one of his questions which wasn't really a question at all, and Eve knew that there was only one answer which was acceptable to them both. For him, because he demanded it and she knew that he had the right to, and for her because her curiosity was roused. 'Okay, I'll meet you,' she said slowly. 'Where?'

'I'll meet you at the Fish Inn at one forty-five.'

'One forty-five,' she echoed.

The journey back seemed to take for ever, and Eve glanced at her watch. There wasn't time to go home first, and besides—what would she go home for? It wasn't like a normal lunch date with a normal man. She was pregnant and about to see the reluctant father. Not a lot of point prettying herself up. And suddenly Eve felt a pang. Luca was a formidable man.

So why the hell was he here?

The Fish Inn was the best restaurant in the village. Simply furnished, serving fresh food and with a stunning view over the harbour—people flocked from miles around to eat there. It was usually impossible to get a table at this short notice, but Luca had somehow managed.

He was already seated when she arrived and his tall, lean body unmistakable. His black hair was ruffled and he wore some beautiful cashmere sweater, the colour of soft, grey clouds, and her heart turned over at the sight of him.

And that is enough, she told herself. More than enough.

He stood up as soon as he saw her, his face looking brooding and shuttered and the dreamy feeling fled, leaving her with a faint feeling of unease.

From behind the lashed curtain of his narrowed eyes, he watched her approach as if his life depended on it. Her face was blooming, he noted with approval, and her eyes were shining with life and with health. She wore dark trousers and a big, soft oatmeal-coloured sweater. Big as a man's sweater, he thought viciously, and felt a stab of anger. But, big as it was, it could not disguise the definite swell of her belly and the anger transmuted into fierce and atavistic pride as he realised that the swell was part of him. His child in her belly. And, to his horror and shock, he felt the early, aching throb of desire.

'Eve,' he said.

He spoke pleasantly, but as he would to some casual acquaintance. It was as if they were oceans apart. There was no kiss on either cheek, no guiding of the arm to her seat. Nothing to treat her in any way as special. In fact, he seemed almost to recoil from her and she wasn't quite sure why that should hurt as much as it did.

'Luca,' she said evenly, and sat down.

'How formal we are with each other,' he mocked softly. 'Why, we speak as strangers, Eve. Who would know, to look at us—that we have made such beautiful love together, and that we have created a child which grows beneath your heart?'

His words were like weapons. *The child beneath her heart.* Didn't that phrase mock her with the tantalising image of what it *could* have been like, if theirs were a normal, loving relationship? And, at the same time, didn't it manage to emphasise just what little there was, or ever had been between them?

Was he trying to wound her, to pay her back?

How calm he looked today, light years away from the man who had stared at her in complete and utter disbelief when she had refused his offer to marry her.

'I don't want to marry you!' she had declared. 'You just want to use marriage to acquire me, and to acquire rights over our baby! Just as you would a business deal!'

He had neither denied nor confirmed it. Just given her a long, considering look and said flatly, 'And that is your decision?'

'It is.'

'Then there is nothing more to be said, is there?'

And the finality of that statement had left her wondering why she hadn't said the most sensible thing, such as: I'd like to think about it, or I'm not ruling anything out. Instead, she was aware that she had burnt her boats, until she reminded herself that her first assessment had been the correct one. She didn't want to marry a man who didn't love her.

With trembling fingers she shook out her linen napkin and laid it carefully over her knees, doubting that she would be able to eat a thing, not with those brilliant black eyes burning into her. But the action composed her, so that she was able to look up at him with a calm expression on her face.

'So,' she said equably. 'You were going to tell me why you were here.'

Did nothing touch her? he wondered furiously. He could be some business acquaintance she was meeting for the first time for all the reaction on her face. What was going on in her mind? In her heart?

For a moment he wished that he had arranged to meet her down by the water, where the foam-flecked grey waters would have drowned his angry words. But he must temper his anger. She carried his child, and although it would have made him feel better to have stormed his rage like the strongest tempest, he must not.

'I saw you on television this morning,' he said unexpectedly.

It was the last thing she had imagined he would say.

'Oh?' she questioned warily.

The waitress came up with her pad, but he waved her away with an impatient hand, then leaned across the table, so close that she could feel the warmth of his breath and see the darkened irises of his eyes which made him look like the devil incarnate.

'You are, as they say, very…telegenic, *cara*,' he drawled.

He made it sound like an insult.

'The camera loves you, doesn't it, Eve?' he continued softly. 'It throws intriguing shadows off those high cheekbones and makes your face look as though it is composed of nothing but those grey-green eyes, like an ocean that a man could drown in.'

The words were like poetry, but he delivered them like a man who didn't want to believe them. 'If that was supposed to be a compliment, then I'll pass on any others,' she said shakily and caught the waitress's eye, gave her a beseeching smile and, thank heavens, she came over.

'I'd like the sole with new potatoes and green beans,' she said steadily. 'And just water to drink. Luca? What would you like?'

If looks could kill, she thought, with a momentary satisfaction.

'I'll have the same,' he said shortly, but inside he was fuming. He was used to a woman letting *him* do the ordering!

Had she done that to demonstrate superiority or equality? A pulse began to beat at his temple and for just one wild, crazy moment he wondered what she would do if he went round to her side of the table and hauled her to her feet and began to kiss her. Would she press her body so eagerly to his, and wind her arms around his neck with the passion she had displayed in such abundance?

'Luca? Are you all right?'

The erotic, frustrating fantasy evaporated and hard on its heels came the sense of burning injustice.

'No, Eve, I am not "all right". In fact, I am angry, very, very angry—probably angrier than I have ever been in my life, but I am doing my best to control it.'

Was he trying to intimidate her? Because he would soon find that she would not be. 'And managing very admirably,' she said sweetly.

'I will not be managing very admirably unless you wipe that smug little smile from your mouth and tell me exactly why you have taken on this new *show*.' The word slid sarcastically from between his lips.

'*Eve in the Morning!*?' she questioned helpfully.

'Eve,' he said warningly. 'I would like some kind of explanation.'

She decided to stop playing games. She was a free agent. He might have claims on the baby, but none on *her* and she was perfectly entitled to live her life as she saw fit.

'I was too sick in the mornings to manage the other ones… Luca, what on earth is the matter?'

'Sick?' he demanded hoarsely. 'You did not tell me you were sick!'

'Of course I didn't—it's quite normal for a pregnant woman to be sick.'

'And the baby?'

Eve softened, because for a moment his face looked so ravaged that she couldn't help it. 'The baby is just fine,' she said gently. 'Honestly. I've seen the doctor and she says that I am as strong as an ox and as fit as a flea and whatever else it is they say about pregnant women!'

And, to his horror, the overriding thought which dominated his mind was his gratitude that she had chosen a woman doctor! If he was not able to watch her naked, growing belly, then he did not want any other man—doctor or not—to be able to.

'So they created this brand-new show, just for me,' she continued.

'So that the whole country is able to participate in your pregnancy! No one is excluded—except, of course, the father!'

'It's regional, Luca—not national—not the *whole* country at all!'

'You are deliberately missing the point,' he said furiously.

Their meals were put down in front of them.

'The point being, what?'

He sighed. To have to admit to feelings he would prefer not to have was something he had never had to do. But Eve was a strong woman, he recognised that. As well as fiercely proud and independent. And stubborn, too. It came as a bolt out of the blue to realise that she did not need him!

'Who knows that I am the father?' he asked suddenly.

Eve didn't answer for a moment.

'Eve?'

Their eyes met. 'I have told only Lizzy,' she admitted. 'Not even Michael—though I expect Lizzy will have done by now.'

She remembered Lizzy's reaction. Her friend had been shocked, but not surprised. 'Can't say I blame you,' she murmured, and then looked at Eve expectantly. 'And?'

Pointless to pretend that she didn't know what that simple one-word question meant. 'It's over,' she said quietly.

Lizzy wasn't able to hide her disappointment. 'And you're happy with that?'

Happy? 'Perfectly happy,' she said brightly.

'Oh, well, that's nice. Very modern!' Then Lizzy leaned forward slightly. 'It's probably all for the best, isn't it? I mean, Michael says that he's well known in the Italian press. Quite a reputation. Though that's hardly surprising, is it? Bad type of man to lose your heart to, Eve!'

'Very bad,' agreed Eve gravely. Please keep telling me these things, Lizzy, she remembered thinking to herself. For these are the things I need to hear.

Luca was staring at her. So she had not announced who the father was! He had expected it to be common knowledge, by now. 'You mean you are ashamed of the child's parentage?' he growled.

'Don't be ridiculous!'

'Then what?'

She put her fork down with a clang. 'Because I wasn't sure if you were going to be around or not and I thought that if you weren't then it would be better for everyone not to know, especially those who didn't need to. I didn't want everyone to be pointing the finger and making value judgements about me.'

He thought how a marriage would have easily solved all such problems, but she had steadfastly refused that.

'You should tell them,' he said. 'Tell everyone or no one, but evade the issue no longer. The child will know, so best that everyone else does.'

'It isn't as easy as that,' she said quietly and met the question in his eyes. 'Because of the job I do, everything in my personal life is considered relevant. That's why I've just said a terse ''no comment'' when people have asked who the father is.'

He swore quietly beneath his breath. 'And you are happy with this?'

Eve shrugged. 'It's the way things are.'

But surely he had the power to change them? He

saw the faint lines of strain around her eyes and decided that now was not the time. 'Eat your lunch!' he instructed gently, and then frowned. 'Have you been eating well, Eve? Properly?'

'Why?'

He frowned. 'You do not look very…pregnant.'

'No. Some women don't—it's the way I carry, apparently.' She thought how seasoned she sounded, as if she had done this a million times before instead of for the first time. And she also thought how *comforting* it was to be able to discuss this kind of thing with someone who cared—and if Luca didn't particularly care for her, he certainly seemed to be making up for it where the baby was concerned.

'So you are eating?' he persisted.

It was also, she discovered, rather nice to have someone who asked her this kind of thing. It was different from when the doctor asked her—that was professional, while this was personal.

She picked up her fork and speared fish and beans and chewed them like an obedient child. 'I am eating like a horse—see! Fish, fruit, vegetables and brown rice—with the occasional portion of cherry ice cream thrown in for good measure!' She gave him a small smile. 'Does that satisfy you?'

He poured some water. Satisfy him? He couldn't ever remember being quite so dissatisfied, both physically and emotionally.

Eve watched him as he lifted his eyes to her, and in them was an expression of respect, though made slightly acid by the wry smile which had curved the kissable lips. He looked so irresistible that she felt a sudden desire to be almost *biddable*…to tell him that it was all going to be all right.

But she didn't know that, and neither could she do it. She was having to fight down the urge to ask him if they couldn't just forget all the events which had brought them to this confusing place and this confusing time and start all over again.

But she couldn't do that either. Too much had happened, and there was a baby on the way. She needed to protect herself against hurt—not just for her sake, but for her baby's sake. A heartbroken mother would not be able to do her job properly.

Yet she wanted to teach her child—their child—all the things which were important, and surely one of the most fundamental was honesty.

'You haven't told me what you feel about this baby, not really,' she said quietly. 'Apart from the anger, of course.'

He remembered how it had devoured him, like a great, burning flame. 'The anger has gone. I should not have reacted so.'

'I guess it was a natural response.' Her eyes were very clear. 'What has replaced it?'

This was difficult for him. He was not a man to put feelings into words, but then this seemed far too important not to, and surely he owed her that. 'Pride,' he said simply. 'And excitement.'

Eve stared at him.

'You look surprised,' he observed.

'That's because I am.' She felt a warm and little protective glow deep within her and she realised how much she valued his pride and his excitement. For the baby's sake.

'And what about you, Eve?' he questioned suddenly. 'What were *your* feelings?' This felt like an uncharted domain. Asking a woman a question like that and actually *caring* what her answer would be.

'I feel excited, too. Yes, very.' And more than a little bit scared, too—if the truth were known. But she would not tell him that. She was a grown woman who had to take responsibility for herself. She was not going to start leaning on Luca.

He nodded, but there was something else he needed to know. 'But not angry?'

She shook her head. 'No. Not anger—I think it expresses itself differently for women. I felt stupid. Trapped.'

'I don't want you to feel trapped.'

'Just what is it that you *do* want, Luca?'

She had asked him this question once before and he had surprised himself by not knowing the answer. This time he did. 'I want to be part of your pregnancy,' he said. 'When you see the doctor, I would like to be there, too. When you have your scans, I want to see my baby's little heart beating.'

Suddenly very emotional, she put her fork down, and stared at her meal, his words making her feel almost unbearably poignant. It took a minute for her to compose herself, and when she looked up again she hoped that he didn't notice that her eyes were bright. He didn't mean it how it sounded. It was intimate, yes, but not truly intimate.

She put on her best, practical voice. 'But how on earth are you going to do that? We live miles apart. I suppose I could send you scans, email you—that kind of thing.'

But he shook his head. 'No, not second hand,' he said firmly.

'How?' she questioned simply.

'Give me enough notice and I can fly over for your appointments.'

'What about your job?'

He looked at her, realising that she had no idea about the nature of his work, but then why would she have? Intellectually, she might be aware that he owned a bank, but she did not live in Italy, she would not know the extent of his power and influence. And since she seemed to have no intention of making any claims on him, he saw no reason not to tell her. It was a curiously liberating feeling not to have to play it down.

'I am rich enough never to have to work again, Eve,' he said softly. 'And certainly in a position to take it easy for a while. I can come and go as I please. I can be there. For the baby.'

And Eve wasn't at all sure how she felt about that.

CHAPTER TEN

LUCA walked into the scanning room and the first things he noticed were the lights. He frowned, his eyes narrowing as they accustomed themselves to the brightness, but the frown deepened as he took in the rest of the small room.

There was Eve, lying on a trolley, with a white-coated technician smearing some thick kind of jelly all over her swollen belly—while a man dressed entirely in denim was swinging a little meter close by.

In one corner, a youngish woman with jangly earrings was in earnest conversation with another man—*another*—who was holding a hand-held camera.

They all looked up as he walked in, and the woman with the jangly earrings smiled and, before Eve could stop her, said, 'I'm sorry—but we're filming in here.'

There was a short, tense silence.

'And what *precisely*,' said Luca, in a voice of dangerous silk, 'do you think you're filming?'

The woman with the jangly earrings stared at him. 'We're doing a feature for a television show, and it's really very crowded in here—so if you wouldn't mind leaving.'

It was exactly like a bomb going off, thought Eve. A deadly little stealth bomb. 'I am not going anywhere,' he grated. 'But I'm afraid that you are. Get out.'

'I'm sorry?'

'You are not, repeat *not*, filming Eve having a scan. Now are you going to leave or do I have to pick up the damn cameras myself and throw them out?'

Jangly earrings looked at Eve. 'Eve?'

She should have been mortified, outraged, and furious with Luca marching in here and single-handedly managing to put her livelihood in jeopardy. But she was none of those things. In theory, the filming of her scan for the show had seemed like a great idea, but the reality was that it had felt intrusive.

And she had never been so glad to see someone in her life.

'Just who *is* this man, Eve?'

'He's…'

'I'm the baby's father,' interjected Luca icily. 'And I want to see the scan of my baby. In *private*.'

There was something about his face and something about the tone of his voice which dared anyone to defy him and the news crew were clearly not going to be the exception.

With much mumbling and clicking of tongues, they packed up their equipment and left, but not before the woman with the jangly earrings had turned to Eve.

'Perhaps you could call me later?'

It took Luca a moment or two to control his breathing, and the white-coated technician was blinking in bemusement.

'And here was me thinking I was going to be on television!' she joked.

Steadying his breathing, Luca shot Eve a look which said 'I will talk to you afterwards' and she felt

exactly like a schoolgirl who had been summoned to
see the headmaster.

But Luca's rage was temporarily forgotten when
the technician began to slide the scanner over the
bump and what had looked like a blur of grey and
black gradually began to seem real.

'There we are,' said the technician. 'Two arms and
two legs—perfect. And there's the heart—can you
see it beating?'

There was silence, only this time a breathless, excited kind of silence.

'Oh, look!' said the technician, as if she hadn't
said this a thousand times before. 'He's sucking his
thumb!'

'He?' shot out Luca.

'Oh, sorry! We always say "he". Habit, really, I
know I shouldn't. Would you like to know your
baby's sex?' she asked casually.

At exactly the same time, Eve and Luca looked
up.

'No,' they said together, their eyes meeting and in
that meeting was a moment of shared and delicious
collusion.

But when the technician had wiped off the con-
ducting jelly and told her to get dressed, Eve began
to feel slightly uneasy. Luca's face was a study in
brooding displeasure. She reached for her trousers.

'I'd better get dressed.'

'I'll wait outside,' said Luca shortly.

As she pulled on her clothes Eve told herself that
she was *not* going to be intimidated by him. She was
not. She could tell that he was mad—hopping mad—
but he had no right to tell her how to run her life.

She sighed as she slithered into a pair of trousers

with difficulty. Things had been going so swimmingly, too. He had behaved like a perfect angel on trips to see the doctor, shamelessly charming her so that the medic had billed and cooed at him with what Eve had thought was quite unprofessional abandon. He flew in at the drop of a hat, as if he were merely travelling from one part of the South Coast to another, and not from another country.

But then he travelled a lot. She knew that because he had told her, in one of his increasingly frequent telephone calls to see how she was.

She had begun to look forward to them. In a way, it was easier talking to him on the phone—then she didn't have to look at his gorgeous dark face or cope with the very real awareness of him as a man, and how her feelings towards him hadn't changed.

Or rather, they had. The attraction she felt for him hadn't, but getting to know him had made her realise what she had always feared, deep down—what she had thought the moment she'd seen him on the other side of the room at Michael and Lizzy's party.

That he was 'the one'.

But that was strictly a one-way street and there was absolutely no point going down there.

He was waiting for her outside in Reception and his face was like thunder.

'Did you bring the car?'

She nodded.

'Give me the keys.'

She handed them over and wondered if she was becoming one of those frightful women who secretly wanted to be dominated. But she reasoned that maybe it was just nice to have someone take over for a change. She yawned.

He didn't say a word when they got in the car, and when they were headed out towards the Hamble he still maintained a simmering silence.

'Luca?'

'Not now, Eve,' he said quietly. 'I am trying very hard to concentrate on driving and if we have this conversation then I am very afraid I won't be able to.'

He waited until they were back in her cottage and then he let rip.

'Are you going to explain what all that was about?'

'You mean the film crew?'

'Please don't play games with me, Eve. You are an intelligent woman—you know exactly what I mean.'

She sat down in one of the armchairs and looked up at him defiantly. 'It's for the programme.'

'Yes, I gathered that much.'

'They wanted to film the scan, that's all.'

'That's *all*?'

She shot a glance at him. 'I don't see what the problem is.'

He gave an angry laugh. 'You don't see what the problem is?' he repeated incredulously. 'What, for half the nation to be staring at your naked stomach!'

'It isn't half the nation,' she began automatically, and then stopped when she saw his face. 'It's supposed to help women see how easy it is,' she tried placatingly.

'And what about the labour itself?' he demanded, hotly. 'Are you going to let a film crew of men film *that*, so that the viewers can see how "easy" it is?'

'No, of course not!'

'Are you sure?'

'Quite sure.' In fact, the idea had actually been mooted at one of the production meetings, but Eve had turned the idea down flat.

'I suppose you think I'm being very old-fashioned.'

'Very.' But wasn't it also protective, and wasn't there some stupid side of her which thrilled to that? It must be the hormones making her react like that.

'I don't want the viewers seeing what is essentially a very private moment. It should be for the mother and father, Eve—for us.'

Except that there was no 'us'. Overwhelmed by an aching sense of longing for what could never be, Eve closed her eyes.

He looked at her. She was pale, he thought, and again a slow, simmering anger began to bubble up. What the hell was she doing, lying there being filmed, her stomach heavy with his child? How had he allowed this to happen? 'I'm going to make some tea,' he said shortly.

She could hear him clattering around in the kitchen, and when he came back in with the tray he was frowning. 'Why were you having a scan at this stage anyway?'

She shrugged listlessly. 'Just routine.'

'Sure?'

She nodded.

He sat down, and picked up her hand, began to stroke it, almost thoughtfully, and Eve's eyes flew open. It was such a little thing. Such a tiny, little thing and yet it felt like heaven. Her body craved comfort and human contact. She met his eyes, wanting above all else for him to take her into his arms, to hold her and to stroke her, but he did not and the dark eyes were thoughtful, watchful, wary.

'For how much longer are you contracted to do this show?' Idly, he circled a finger over her hand.

She swallowed. Don't stop touching me, she thought. 'It finishes on the third.'

'That's next week.'

She nodded.

'And then?'

'Then I'm on maternity leave. I'll look at other options when...when I've had the baby.'

'Eve.' He paused. 'Are you happy with what you're doing?'

'You mean the show?'

'That is part of it. But your life here. What you see for the future. Just what *do* you see for the future, *cara mia*?'

It was a long time since he had called her that, and it made her want to weep with longing. For what it might have been. For what it was not.

'It's like I jumped onto a merry-go-round and I can't get off,' she admitted slowly, and at that moment she didn't care if she sounded vulnerable. She *felt* vulnerable—and pregnant women were allowed to, weren't they? She was fed up with being brave and strong and coping. She *did* want to lean on Luca, if not emotionally, then at least practically. Just for a little. To pretend that he would really always be there for her...

'As for the future—well, it isn't something that I gave much thought to before. But now...' Her voice tailed off.

'Now?' he prompted.

'I realise that I have to. And I just don't know any

more. Oh, Luca!' And to her horror, tears began to slide from her eyes. She bit her lip and tried to stop them, but she could not and it was as though she had been teetering on a knife-edge of control as she began to cry.

An expression of pain crossed his face. Had he pushed her so far to cause her this? He pulled her into his arms and began to smooth his hand down over the silken mane of her hair, over and over again in a soothing and comforting rhythm. 'Shh. Don't cry, Eve. Don't cry, *cara mia*. No need for tears. Everything is going to be fine, I promise you.'

Her tear-wet cheek was buried in his neck. She could smell the raw maleness of him and feel the warmth which radiated from him. His arms were tight and strong and protective. Nothing could hurt her here. At least, no outside forces could—her ache in her heart was the most dangerous thing she had to fear.

She drew away from him, wiping her cheeks with the back of her hand. 'I'm sorry,' she sniffed.

'Don't be sorry.' He touched away a last stray tear with the tip of his finger. How shocked would she be if he told her that a part of him liked seeing her weak, like this? For her weakness meant that his own strength could come to the fore, and wasn't that the way he liked it best? 'What would happen if you told them you didn't want to go back to work? At least for the foreseeable future?'

'It would probably be the end of my career. Viewers have very short memories and even shorter loyalties.'

'Yes, your career. *Your damned career*,' he said softly. 'What's going to happen when the baby is born, Eve? Who will look after our son or our daughter when that car whisks you away to the studio every day?'

She looked at him. He was still so close, close enough to kiss, but she did not dare. 'I don't know anything any more,' she whispered. 'I don't even know how much I care about my career.' Her eyes glittered defiantly. 'I suppose you think that's a shocking admission?'

It was the best thing he had heard her say in a long time, but he was clever enough not to say so. 'Why should it be?'

She shrugged, thinking that the woman he had been attracted to was the smart, able career woman. 'I guess I think that my job defines me.'

'No job should define a person. And you haven't answered my question,' he persisted. 'What's going to happen when the baby is born?'

'I don't have a choice. I have to work.'

'But that's just the point, Eve—you *do* have a choice. You can come back to Italy with me. As my wife.'

There was a long, breathless silence.

'You don't mean that.'

'I never say anything I don't mean. But believe me when I tell you that I will not ask you again.'

She sat back against the cushions. 'Why? I mean—really?'

'Truthfully?' He rubbed his finger along the shadowed line of his chin. 'I would like the child to be born in Italy, and I want to see that child grow up.'

At least he hadn't told her lies. Told her that he loved her and couldn't live without her. 'You think those are good enough reasons for getting married?'

she asked, and her voice was trembling in a way that didn't sound like her at all.

'I can't think of any better,' he said simply. 'What is the alternative? That you bring up the baby here, alone.' His eyes darkened. 'Or maybe not alone. Think what you like of me, Eve—but the thought of another man bringing up my child as his own sickens me to the stomach.'

She nodded. Oh, yes, she could see that. They were qualities of possessiveness and ownership, certainly, but at least he had had the guts to admit it. He wasn't to know that the situation would never arise and she wasn't going to tell him that no man would feature in her life, not after him. For who could hold a candle to Luca Cardelli?

And the flip-side to his not being able to stand the thought of another man was the spectre of Luca being with another woman. Could she bear that? Imagine if Luca married someone else, and she had to send the child to stay with them, weekends and holidays and, worse, alternate Christmases? Another woman being a stepmother to her child. If there were qualities of ownership and possession, then Eve was just discovering that Luca didn't have a monopoly on them.

Shouldn't she give what they had—however precarious—a chance? Rather than risk time and distance making them grow further and further apart, so that it didn't become a case of *if* he got another woman, but *when*.

She thought of what he was offering her. 'It's more than just marriage, though,' she pointed out thoughtfully. 'It's a whole new life in a whole new country.'

'An adventure! A beautiful country, and a beautiful city.' His eyes glittered and his voice softened to rich velvet. 'I could so easily make you fall in love with my city, Eve.'

She didn't doubt it for a moment. He had managed to make her fall in love with *him* without even trying. But Luca was a passionate man, and there was an aspect to marriage he hadn't even touched. The aspect which had turned everything upside down, including their lives.

'When you say...marriage...'

He saw the way she bit her lip. 'You are afraid that I am going to start demanding my "rights"?' he mocked softly.

'Well, are you?' It should have been a teasing response and if it had been then who knew how he might have reacted? But, as it was, it came out more like a sulky little question and hung on the air like an accusation.

A pulse began to beat at his temple. 'I will demand nothing of you, Eve,' he retorted silkily. 'If that's what you're worried about.'

Could it be any more complicated than it was? she wondered. What had happened had put up barriers between them, of course it had. Luca had shown no sign of wanting to make love to her ever since she had first told him that she was pregnant. At first she had put it down to his anger, but now that the anger had gone he still hadn't gone near her. Which could mean that he no longer found her physically attractive.

Yet there were times when she caught him looking at her with a hot and hungry look in his eyes which made her think that perhaps he did. Though it was different for men, she knew that. They responded automatically to a woman sometimes—though, considering her current state of swollen ankles and swollen belly, she might simply have imagined it.

And now he said he would demand nothing of her. Did that mean that he expected *her* to make the first move? And how could she—so lumberingly and unattractively pregnant—make an overture towards him which he might then reject? Or maybe he wouldn't demand because he didn't want her in that way, not any more.

'You're having second thoughts?' he mused.

'I haven't even got through the first ones yet.'

He laughed then and it was the laugh that did it. To have the ability to make a man like Luca laugh surely meant something. She loved him and she was expecting his baby and he had offered to marry her. What was not to accept? What was to make her cling onto what she had here—a job which had become increasingly unimportant when compared to the enormity of bringing new life into the world?

She smiled. 'What type of wedding did you have in mind?'

CHAPTER ELEVEN

As IT was, with all the arrangements to be made, it was close onto a month before the wedding could take place, and by then she was almost up to the limit of when it was safe to fly.

There was a licence to be obtained, a dress to buy and a simple reception to be organised.

Though her choice of wedding dress was strictly limited by her physical dimensions.

'You look lovely,' sighed Lizzy.

'Liar! I look like a whale!'

'Well, you don't, and even if you did—who cares, when you're getting married to Luca?' sighed Lizzy. 'He obviously loves you whatever you look like!'

Eve didn't like to disillusion her. What would have been the point? She had taken Lizzy up to London with her, where, armed with a ridiculous amount of money, she had persuaded a hot, up-and-coming young fashion designer to try to work magic with her appearance. The result was a coat-dress, cleverly cut to disguise the bump, in fine cashmere of the softest, palest ivory. An outrageous hat had been made to match. 'It'll naturally draw the eye to your face,' said the designer. 'Which is just *glowing* with pregnancy!'

A bouquet which was luscious and extravagant enough to cover the bump completed the ensemble. In fact, the whole outfit was an illusory one, thought Eve as she twirled in front of the floor-length mirror.

Something made to look like something it wasn't—
and maybe an accurate reflection of the marriage itself.

Still, she had agreed to go through with it, and she
would do so with all her heart.

The day after she had accepted Luca's proposal
she had gone into work and told them. And unfortunately someone had phoned the local press.

EVE IS THE APPLE OF ITALIAN'S EYE! reported the
South Hampshire daily.

'In a way, I admire you,' Clare told her, a touch
enviously. 'Giving all this up for love. And marriage.'

And Eve didn't have the heart to disillusion her,
either.

On her final broadcast, she explained that she was
getting married and moving to Rome.

'Why, you looked positively wistful when you
said that, *cara*,' drawled Luca, who had watched the
show. 'So was that genuine, or just good acting?'

Did he think of her as an actress, then? Able to
hide her emotions behind a veneer of professional-
ism? And if so, wasn't that a skill which might prove
useful in the ensuing months?

The wedding took place in the Hamble, in the
yacht club where she had first seen Luca. A girl of
about the same age as Eve had served them champagne and Dublin Bay prawns and Eve thought how
heartbreakingly young she looked.

It was a small affair with Lizzy and Michael, and
Kesi as bridesmaid, and Luca's sister Sophia had
flown over, leaving her husband with her baby back
at home. Eve had felt nervous about meeting her, but

she was strung out with nerves anyway, and thought how faraway her voice sounded during the ceremony.

She felt strange, as if it were all happening to someone else, as if she were in a bubble which protected her from the rest of the world. And although her heart ached with love and longing, the vows they exchanged seemed to have no real meaning because they didn't really mean *anything*. Certainly not to Luca.

It was ironic in a way that she, who had always considered herself a very modern woman, should be entering into a very old-fashioned marriage of convenience.

Luca took her in his arms afterwards, briefly brushing his lips over hers in a kiss which didn't mean anything either, for there was no promise in it. Not for them the usual passion of the newly-weds, only restrained by social niceties, just a perfunctory kiss to make it look as everyone thought it should look.

'You look very beautiful,' he murmured.

But what bride could possibly feel beautiful at such an advanced state of pregnancy?

Yet Sophia had hugged Eve like a sister, and run her hand over the bump in a delighted way which spoke of pride, rather than something to be ashamed of. 'Stand up to him,' she had said, when rose petals and rice had flown off on the wind towards the water. 'He has had too much of his own way for all his life. And I'll see you in Rome, once you are settled, *sì*?'

Settled?

Eve wasn't sure that she would ever feel settled again, and when they arrived at the front of Luca's apartment she felt the very opposite as he turned to her, his dark eyes glittering.

'Shall I carry you over the threshold, Eve?'

'Is that an Italian custom, as well as an English one?' she said breathlessly.

He smiled. 'It is indeed. Come.'

And he scooped her up in his arms and carried her into the apartment.

'Put me down, I'm too heavy,' she protested.

'Not for me,' he demurred.

No. He was a strong man and Eve wondered if he could feel or hear the thundering of her heart. It was, she realised, the closest they had been for a long time. With one hand beneath her knees and the other locked around her expanded waistline and her leaning against his chest. She could smell the raw, feral masculine scent of him, feel his hard body as it tensed beneath her weight.

If this had been a real wedding, he would carry her straight into the bedroom and lay her down and slowly undress her and make love until the morning light came up.

But it was not, and he did not. Instead, he put her carefully down in the centre of the vast, spacious sitting room as if she were some delicate and precious container, which was exactly, she guessed, how he saw her. For she carried within her his child, and nothing could be more precious than that to the man who had everything else.

The undrawn curtains framed the stunning beauty of the night lights of Rome, though she was blind to it. All she could see and sense was him. He was still wearing the dark and elegant suit he had worn for the wedding, though she had insisted on changing from her wedding finery for the journey home.

'It's more comfortable this way,' she had explained in answer to his silent look of query as she'd appeared in a trousers and a pink silk tunic, which by no stretch of the imagination could be classified as a 'going-away' suit. But it was more than that. She hadn't thought she could bear to go through the charade of people congratulating her, them—making a fuss of her on the flight, behaving as if they really were a pair of exquisitely happy newly-weds, when nothing could have been further from the truth.

His eyes had narrowed. 'So be it, *cara*,' he had said softly. 'Comfort is, of course, essential.'

And now they were here, and she was ready to begin her new life and she didn't even know what the sleeping arrangements would be.

He saw the wary look on her face. Like a cornered animal, he thought grimly. Was she afraid that he would drag her to the bedroom—insist on consummating this strange marriage of theirs?

'Would you like to see your room?'

Well, that told her. 'I'd love to!' she said brightly. 'I'm so tired I think I could sleep for a whole century!'

'A whole century?' he echoed drily.

In any other time or in any other situation, Eve would have exclaimed with delight at the bedroom he took her to. It was perfect. A room full of light, furnished in creams and softest peach.

But Eve had seen *his* bedroom. Had shared that vast bed of his, where tonight he would sleep alone. For one brief and impetuous moment she almost turned to him, to put her hand on his arm and say shyly that she would prefer to spend the night with him. But he had moved away to draw the blinds, and part of her was relieved, knowing that if they made love it would change everything—it would shatter what equilibrium she had and make her vulnerable in a way she simply couldn't afford to be. And there were far too many other things going on to risk that.

He turned back from the blinds, and the blocked-out night made the light in the room dim, throwing his tall, lean figure into relief so that he looked dark and shadowy, like an unknown man in an unknown room in an unknown city.

And that, she thought painfully, was exactly the way it was.

'Goodnight, Eve,' he said softly.

'Goodnight, Luca.'

'Do you have everything you need?'

No. 'Yes. Thank you.'

She stood exactly where she was, listening to the sounds of Luca moving around, until at last she heard the sound of his bedroom door closing quietly, and it was like a sad little signal.

Sighing as she looked at her brand-new, shiny wedding ring, she began to get undressed.

But when she woke up in the morning and drew open the blinds, she sucked in a breath of excitement at the sight of the city which lay beneath her, and it changed and lifted her mood. It couldn't fail to. It was like a picture-postcard view, she thought. And there was so much to discover.

She showered and dressed and wandered into the kitchen to find the tantalising aroma of good coffee and Luca squeezing oranges, a basket of newly baked bread on the table.

He gave her a slightly rueful look. 'I hope this is okay?'

She sat down, suddenly hungry. 'It looks wonderful.' She remembered the time when she had stayed with him, exclaiming that his fridge had been completely bare, save for two bottles of champagne and a tin of caviare. And he had taken her out to a nearby café for breakfast, explaining that he never ate in.

'You've taken to eating breakfast at home now, then?' she questioned as she poured her coffee.

'I shopped for these first thing,' he said, feeling like a man who had accomplished a mission impossible! 'I guess things are going to have to change around here.'

Automatically, her hand crept to her stomach. 'Well, er, yes,' she said drily.

He laughed. 'Homes have food, so I guess I'm going to have to learn how to shop. And cook.'

Eve laughed. He wore the expression of a man who had just announced his intention to wade through a pit of snakes. 'If you shop—I'm happy to cook.'

'You cook?'

She gave him a look of mock reprimand. 'Of course I cook! I love cooking.' She risked it. 'I could teach you, if you like.'

A woman teaching him!

'You might not be able to stand taking orders from a woman, of course,' she said shrewdly.

He met her eyes. 'Oh, I think I could bear taking orders from you, Eve.'

She hastily broke the warm, fragrant bread. She was going to have to watch herself, if some simple, throwaway comment like that was going to have her heart racing with some completely disproportionate pleasure, as if he had just offered her the moon and the stars.

He sat down opposite her, feeling oddly relaxed. It felt strange to be eating breakfast with a woman in his own home and not covertly glancing at his watch and wondering how soon he could get his own space back.

'I've made you an appointment to see an obstetrician tomorrow morning,' he said, and then added, 'He's the best in the city.'

She supposed that went without saying. Everything that was the best would now be hers for the taking, and she must try to appreciate it. Not get bogged down with wanting everything to be perfect, because nothing ever was, everyone knew that.

'And I think we might arrange a small party—that way you can get to meet everyone at once—what do you think?'

It was her first real entrée into his life. A whole circle of Luca's smart and sophisticated friends—how were *they* going to accept her? She hadn't even put that into part of the equation. 'What will they think?'

He raised his eyebrows in faintly insolent query. 'That you're my wife and that you're expecting my baby—what else is there for them to think?'

He was right. Even if it had been a conventional love marriage, he would not have gone around telling his friends so. They would just have made the assumption. Would they notice that he didn't touch her? That they behaved as benignly as two flatmates? She stirred her coffee. 'Luca.'

He let his eyes drift over her. Her hair was loose

and the morning light was spilling over it. He had never seen so many different hues in a head of hair and it looked like molasses and honey with warm hints of amber. Her green-grey eyes were bright and clear, their lashes long and curling even though she wasn't wearing a scrap of make-up. She looked wholesome and clean and healthy, he thought, and that, surprisingly, was incredibly sexy. He hadn't slept a wink last night, imagining her in the bed next door to his. What, he wondered, was she wearing in bed at the moment? Did pregnant women feel the need to cover up? He shifted slightly. 'Mmm?'

'I'd like to learn Italian, please. And as soon as possible.'

He heard the determination in her voice. It didn't surprise him, but it pleased him. 'All my friends speak English,' he commented. 'Spanish, too.'

'Yes. Yes, I sort of somehow imagined that they would.'

'And the baby is going to take a while to learn how to speak!' he teased.

'Yes, I know that, too! But I don't want to be one of those women who move to another country and lets her...her...husband do all the talking for her.' The word sounded strange on her lips. As if she were a fraud for saying it.

'I can't imagine you letting *anyone* do the talking for you, Eve,' he said drily. 'But, of course, I will arrange for a tutor for you. That might be better than going out to a class, particularly at the moment, don't you think?'

She nodded. How easy it was to arrange and talk about practical things. And how easy to suppress feelings and emotions. To put them on the back-boiler so that they didn't disturb the status quo.

'It seems strange to think of our baby talking,' he said slowly.

'Too…too far in the future to imagine?' she questioned tentatively.

'A little. But I was just thinking that his or her first language will be English, won't it? The mother tongue.' He thought then of the reality of what her being here meant. Or rather, what it would have been like if she had stayed in England. He wouldn't have got a look-in, not really. It would have been false and unreal and ultimately frustrating and unrewarding. Suddenly, he understood some of the sacrifice it must have taken for her to have come here—to start all over in a territory which was completely unknown to her.

'We'll need to think about decorating a room,' he mused.

'Pink, or blue?' She searched his face. What if secretly he was so macho that he would only be satisfied with a son—and what if she didn't produce one, what then? 'Which would you prefer, a boy or a girl?'

He frowned, as if the question had surprised him.

'I don't care which; there is only one thing I care about.'

'Yes.' Their eyes met and she smiled. 'A healthy baby. It's what every parent prays for.' She looked at him. 'So it's yellow?'

'Yellow? *Sì. Giallo.*' A smile creased the corners of his eyes. 'Say it after me.'

She felt giddy with the careless innocence of it. *'Gi-allo.'*

'So, there is your first Italian lesson!' He leaned back indolently in his chair and studied the lush breasts through narrowed eyes. 'What would you like to do today? The Grand Tour of the city?'

She thought about it. What she wanted and craved more than anything was some kind of normality, for there had been precious little of it in her life of late. And even if such a thing were too much to hope for, she needed to start living life as she—or rather, they—meant to go on.

'Will you show me round the immediate vicinity?' she asked. Would something like that sound prosaic to such an urbane and cosmopolitan man? 'Show me where the nearest shops are. Where I can buy a newspaper, that kind of thing. We could—if you meant it—go and buy some stuff for supper? Is there somewhere close by?'

He nodded. 'There is the *al mercato di Campo de Fiori* and there are shops. Sounds good.'

She hesitated. She knew something of his lifestyle—the man with nothing in the fridge who rarely ate in, who travelled the world and went to fancy places. 'Luca?'

'Eve?' he said gravely.

She drew a breath. 'Listen, I know you're usually out—probably every night for all I know. You mustn't stay in just because of me.'

'You mean you want to go out at night?'

'Like this?' She shook her head, and laughed. 'I'm far too big and lumbering to contemplate hitting on Rome's top night-spots!'

He frowned. 'You mean you want me to go out without you?'

'If you want to. I just want you to know that I

don't intend to cramp your style. You mustn't feel tied—because of the baby.'

He stared at her. Did she have a degree in psychology, or just a witch's instinct for knowing how to handle a man? That by offering him his freedom, he now had no desire to take it!

'I am no longer a boy,' he said gravely. 'And "top night-spots" kind of lost their allure for me a long time ago. So I'll stay in. With you.'

'Sure you won't be bored?'

'Let's wait and see.'

Her voice was wry. 'That seems to be a recurrent theme with us, doesn't it?'

'Indeed.' Their eyes met. He admired her mind, he realised, and her sense of humour, too. The baby was going to be a lucky baby to have her as a mother, he thought suddenly. 'I'm glad you're here, Eve,' he said.

She put her coffee-cup down with a hand which was trembling. But he was merely being courteous, and he should be offered the same in return. She smiled. 'And so am I.'

CHAPTER TWELVE

'WE'RE not going to cook every night,' said Luca suddenly, one morning.

Eve didn't answer for a moment. The baby's foot was sliding across the front of her belly and she sat and watched it, then lifted her head. 'You mean last night was a disaster?'

He shook his head. The simple meal they had eaten on the terrace beneath the stars had been almost perfect. Almost. She was engaging and stimulating company and, because sex was off limits, all the focus had been on the conversation and this was new territory for him.

Luca wasn't averse to talking to women but he usually regarded conversation with them as purely functional. You might talk to a woman if you were dealing with her at work. Or if you were flirting with her, or making pleasant small talk before taking her to bed, or chatting to the wives of friends. They were easier to talk to, in a way, because they had no expectations of you as a potential partner, which all other women did.

But he was a man's man—he rarely had conversation with a woman for conversation's sake. With Eve he had to—and last night he had realised why she had been so successful at her job. He had persuaded her to talk about her work, something she was normally reluctant to do.

He had understood for the first time that working

in television was not easy and that the skill lay in making it *look* easy. Not many people could cope with live and unpredictable interviews, while at the same time having the studio crew sending frantic instructions into your earpiece.

'Will you ever want to go back to it?' he had persisted.

In Italy? With a baby? Who knew *what* she would want—and did people ever get what they truly wanted? Protected still by the bubble of pregnancy which surrounded her, Eve had smiled. 'We'll see.'

Luca stared at her, watching the dreamy way that she observed the baby's movements. 'No, Eve, it was not a disaster.'

Disaster was too strong a word. Crazy was better.

It seemed crazy that they should part at the end of the evening and go off to sleep in their separate beds. Or rather, for him to toss and turn and think about how pregnancy could make a woman seem so intensely beautiful. Like a ripe and juicy peach.

He wanted to lie with her. Not to make love—something deep within him told him that it would be entirely inappropriate to consummate their marriage when she was heavy with his child. But he would have liked to have held her. To have wrapped her in his arms and smoothed the silken splendour of her hair. To have run his fingertips with possessive and wondrous freedom over the great curve of her belly.

'It is just that your freedom, and mine—will be restricted by a baby.'

'Only a few weeks now,' she observed serenely.

'Exactly! Time to make the most of what we have, while we still have it! We shall play the tourist.'

'I suppose when you put it *that* way,' Eve murmured. Maybe they should get out more. Heaven only knew, it was difficult enough to be this close to him and not close enough to him. Itching for him to touch her, to kiss her—anything which might give her some inkling of whether or not he still found her sexually attractive, or whether that had died a death a long time ago.

He showed her a different side of Rome. Took her to all the secret places of his boyhood, the dark, hidden crevices and sunlit corners.

'We aren't really playing the tourist at all, are we?' she asked him as they strolled slowly around a hidden garden, soft with the scent of roses. 'No tourist would ever find places as hidden away as these are.'

'Ah, but this is the true Rome. For Romans.'

Eve felt a brief, momentary pang of isolation. Their child would grow up and learn this secret Rome, with a native's knowledge which would always elude her.

'Eve?' said Luca softly. 'What is it?'

I'm frightened of what the future holds, she wanted to say to him. But she wouldn't. She had to learn to cope and deal with her own fears—not project them onto Luca. 'Nothing,' she said softly.

They dined with Patricio, Luca's oldest friend and his wife, Livvy, who went out of their way to make her feel comfortable. Livvy had a toddler about the same age as Kesi and Eve was glad that all Luca's friends weren't childless.

Gradually, she began to relax.

And then, one starlit evening, they were walking home after having late-night coffee and pastries and Eve suddenly stopped, drawing in a gasp as a terrible sharp spasm constricted across her middle. 'Ouch!'

Luca caught her by the arm. 'What is it?'

She could see the paling of his face and shook her head. 'It was nothing. It must have been the cake that… Oh, Luca…Luca—it hurts!'

'*Madre de Dio!*' he swore and steadied her. 'I *said* we should get a taxi!' He held up his hand and a taxi screeched to do his bidding as if it had been lurking round the corner, just waiting for his command.

Eve's Italian was still pretty non-existent, but even she understood the word '*ospedale*'. 'Luca, I am *not* going to hospital!'

'*Sì, cara,*' he contradicted grimly. 'You are!'

She stared him out. 'No,' she said stubbornly. 'And anyway, the baby isn't due for another two weeks. I want to go home!'

His impotent fury that she could not and would not be persuaded—he could tell that from the stubborn set of her mouth—was softened slightly by her instinctive use of the word 'home'. He nodded. 'Very well,' he agreed softly. 'We will go home. But the doctor will visit, and he will decide.' He saw her open her mouth to protest. '*He will decide, Eve,*' he said, in a voice which broached no argument.

'It's a waste of his time!'

But Eve was wrong and Luca and the doctor were right. It was not a false alarm. The baby was on the way.

Everything became a fast and frantic blur, punctuated only by sharp bursts of pain which became increasingly unbearable.

'I want an epidural!' she gasped as they wheeled her into the delivery room.

But it was too late for an epidural, too late for anything. She was having her baby and the midwife was saying something to her frantically, something she didn't understand.

'*Spinga, signora! Spinga, ora!*'

'*Luca*! I'm so scared! What is she saying?'

'She is saying, push, *cara*. And you must not be scared. Trust me, I am here with you.'

'Oh! Ow!'

She gripped his hands, her fingernails tearing into his flesh, but he scarcely noticed. 'You're doing fine,' he coaxed. 'Just fine.' He snapped something rapid in Italian at the midwife, who immediately began speaking in slow, fractured English.

'One more push, *signora*. One more. Take a deep breath and…'

'Now, *cara*!' urged Luca softly as he saw something in her face begin to change. '*Now!*'

Eve pulled her hand away from his, her head falling back as she made one last, frantic little cry and Luca moved just in time to see his baby being born.

'Here's your baby,' said the midwife and she deftly caught the infant.

He stared. A little wet black head and a long, slithery body. The world seemed to stand still as the midwife sprang into action, cutting the cord, wiping a plug of mucus from the little nose.

Eve half sat up in bed, her damp hair plastered all over her face, watching the midwife as if nothing else on the planet existed right then.

For one long and breathless moment, there was silence, and then the infant opened its lungs and let out a baleful and lusty cry and Eve burst into tears of relief as the midwife held it up triumphantly.

'You have a son, *signore, signora*!' and she swaddled him in a blanket and placed him straight on Eve's breast.

Luca turned away, feeling the unfamiliar taste of tears at the back of his throat, but Eve needed strength now, not weakness. He sucked in a deep breath as he tried to compose himself. He had watched her suffer, had heard her cry out in pain and seen the fear on her face as the overwhelming spasms had brought the baby from her body. For the first time in his life he had been helpless, the experience of it all making everything else he had seen in his life somehow insignificant, but that should not really surprise him. For this was a miracle. Truly, a miracle.

Joyfully, Eve stared down at the baby as it suckled from her breast and she glanced over at Luca, but he was staring out of the window. She needed him right now, but her needs were no longer paramount. And suddenly nothing else seemed to matter. Motherhood had kicked in.

She studied the tiny creature intently. 'Hello, baby,' she said softly. 'Hello, Oliviero. Oliviero Patricio.' Funny how the name they had chosen seemed to suit him perfectly. She put her finger out and a tiny little fist curled round it. Maybe because everything about him was perfect.

Luca turned round, still shaken, and stared at the tableau the two of them made. The child suckled at her breast and she was making soft little cooing sounds. She looked like a Madonna, he thought—as if the two of them had created their own magic circle, excluding the world and all others.

Didn't men sometimes say that they felt excluded when a baby was born? And that was when the relationship was as it should be. His mouth tightened, and he felt bitterly ashamed at the selfishness of his thoughts. Eve had given birth to a beautiful son, he thought. His son. And his heart turned over.

Eve saw him watching her, and felt suddenly shy, unsure how to deal with these big, new emotions. 'Would you…would you like to hold him?' she asked.

'He's not still hungry?'

The midwife laughed. 'A child of this size will always be hungry! Hold him, *signore*—let him know who his father is!'

Luca had always held his nephew with a kind of confident ease, but this felt completely different. He bent down and Eve carefully deposited the precious bundle into his arms.

She watched the two of them, transfixed by the sight of the strong, powerful man held in thrall to the tiny baby.

Luca looked down and his son opened his eyes and stared up at him, and in that moment his heart and his soul connected. 'I will die for him,' he said fiercely, hardly aware that he had spoken aloud. 'My little Oliviero Patricio.'

Eve lay back on the pillows, and the enormity of what had happened slammed home to her in a way it hadn't before. She had been protected by the slight sense of unreality which pregnancy gave you, which made you sometimes feel you weren't part of the outside world.

Hadn't part of her always thought that if it didn't work out, they would quietly divorce and she could slip back to England? But now she knew that would never happen. The possessive pride which had softened Luca's hard, handsome face told her that. He would die for him, he had said, and he would fight for him, too. She knew that. Whichever way she looked at it—as a gilded prison, or a marriage of convenience—she had better make the best of it, because she was here now for the duration.

She closed her eyes. She was weary now.

They took Oliviero home six days later, to a flat where Luca had clearly been busy. There were flowers everywhere—roses and lilies and tulips—colourful and scented, and more than a little overwhelming. The yellow nursery was filled with balloons, and there was a pile of cards, waiting, and gifts wrapped exquisitely in blue and silver and blue and gold. It looked as if a Hollywood film star were about to pay a visit and Eve found it all a little overwhelming.

And the lift journey up to the penthouse only served to remind her that this was essentially a bachelor's flat. She thought of the pristine white walls and the frosted glass and shuddered as her mind tried to make the connection with a rampaging toddler.

Luca carried the baby in and placed the carry-cot on the coffee-table, smiling at him tenderly before looking up at Eve.

'He sleeps well,' he observed softly. 'You feed him well, Eve.'

Stupidly, she found herself blushing and turned away. It seemed such an intimate thing for him to say, and yet what could be more intimate than the fact he had witnessed the birth? He had seen her at her most naked and vulnerable, stripped and defenceless and in a way that was scary.

Luca noted the way she wouldn't look at him, and his eyes narrowed. So be it. If distance was what she wanted, then distance was what she would get.

'Are you hungry?' he questioned.

Her instinct was to say no, but she knew she had to eat. She nodded. 'I think I might have a bath first.'

'That's fine,' he said coolly. 'Sit down, and I'll run one for you.'

She had offended him and she didn't know why. 'No, honestly—'

'Eve, sit down,' he repeated, rather grimly. 'You have been through a lot.'

Rather gingerly, she sat down, gazing at Oliviero as he lay sleeping so peacefully, listening to the sound of water rushing into the bath.

'It's ready.'

She looked up. Luca was standing there, silhouetted by the door, looking dark and edgy and somehow formidable. It would have been strange fitting into these new roles of mother and father whatever the circumstances, but the distance between them only seemed to make them stranger. A distance she didn't quite know how, or if, she could ever breach.

Slowly, she got to her feet. Still at that new-mother-scared stage of not wanting to let him out of her sight, she fixed him with an anxious look. 'You'll keep an eye on Oliviero?'

His eyes hardened. What did she think he was going to do? Take a stroll around the piazza and leave him? 'Sure,' he said shortly.

She couldn't remember ever seeing him quite so keyed up. Maybe it was the birth of a baby. It was a stressful time for a man, too—she mustn't forget that.

But the bath made her feel a million times better and so did the hair-wash. Through the soapy and bubbly water she looked down at her stomach, which seemed amazingly flat. Of course, it wasn't flat at all compared to its normal state, but it wasn't too bad, considering. The midwife had told her that she was going to be one of those lucky few who would be back in her jeans within the month, and Eve hoped so.

She had eaten healthily and carefully throughout the pregnancy and she didn't want to let herself go. For her sake, but also because of the sophisticated and sylph-like women in Luca's circle of friends.

And for Luca's sake? prompted a little voice in her head. Don't you want t keep your body looking good for him? She let the water out and stepped out of the bath, the droplets drying on her skin.

She stared at her face in the mirror. What happened now? Would Luca attempt to make her his wife in the most fundamental way now that there was no baby inside her? Not tonight, that was for sure— but in the days to come?

She pulled on some velvet trousers and hid their elasticated waist with a long, silky shirt in a shade of deep green which brought out the natural green in her eyes. She blasted her hair with the dryer and fussed around with it and stood back from the mirror, quite pleased with her reflection.

And when she came out from the bathroom it was to see that Luca had set the table and she blinked in surprise to see that it was lit by candlelight. There was salad and pasta and a dish of figs and white peaches.

And a bottle of champagne cooling.

Her mouth feeling suddenly dry with nerves, Eve sat down.

'That looks…very nice,' she said weakly.

He glanced up from tearing the foil from the bottle. He saw her eyes stray nervously to the wine. Did she think he was trying to lull her into letting her guard down?

His mouth hardened as he poured the champagne into two goblets and he handed her one.

'What shall we drink to?' said Eve. To love? she thought ironically as she saw the cynical curve of his mouth. To happy ever after?

'To our son. To Oliviero.'

Of course. 'To Oliviero.' She raised her goblet to mirror his and as their glasses touched she thought she had never heard a colder sound.

'It is good to be home?' he said carefully.

Eve took a huge mouthful as she looked around the room which had his beautiful and rather austere taste stamped all over it, wondering if it would ever truly feel like *her* home, as well as his. Wistfully, she remembered that glorious weekend she had spent here, when they had been unencumbered by anything except the sheer pleasure of the moment. It seemed like another lifetime ago, but in a way she supposed that it was.

She wondered how many different women had sat here, just where she was sitting now. Drinking champagne as a precursor to going to that vast bed of his and being made love to for the rest of the night.

But she would go off alone to her creamy, peachy bedroom and he would go off alone to his.

And the irony was that she was his wife!

She took the question at face value. 'It's good to be out of hospital,' she said carefully.

'That good, huh?' he mocked.

'I didn't mean it how it sounded.'

'Don't worry about it, Eve,' he said. 'It's bound to be strange.'

Frustratedly, she took another sip of the champagne. It was cold and dry and delicious and it seemed to dull some of the empty, aching feeling inside her. Dangerous to drink on an empty stomach. Alcohol loosened the inhibitions and who knew what she might then blurt out? She put the glass down and reached for the food instead.

She wished that he wouldn't just sit there like that, watching her from the narrowed dark eyes as if she were some kind of specimen in a test-tube, some new and undiscovered species. Maybe that was it. Maybe he just wasn't sure how to treat the woman who had just had his baby who was his wife, but in name only. Come to think of it, she thought slightly giddily—she couldn't blame him. There certainly wasn't a rule-book he could look up for guidelines on how to cope with such a situation.

'When will you have to go back to work?' she asked him.

'Whenever I please. I want to make sure that you're happy and settled before I do.'

Happy and settled. If only he knew. She wondered what had happened to the old Eve—who could chat and banter and tease him and feel like an equal to him. Had she been left on the shores of her native land, been cast off with her life as a single mother? 'That's very sweet of you.'

Luca had been described in many ways by women during his life, but 'sweet' had never been one of them. He did not want to be 'sweet'. He made an impatient little noise as he got up from the table and drew something from the back pocket of his jeans, a slim, navy leather box, and he put it on the table in front of Eve, as casually as he would a deck of cards.

Her heart was beating very fast. Everyone knew what came in boxes which looked like that.

'Wh-what's this?'

'Why not open it, and see?'

She flipped the lid off and drew in a breath of disbelief to see a bracelet glittering against the navy velvet. A band of iridescent, sparkling diamonds, each one as big as a fingernail. She stared at it, then looked up at him in genuine horror.

'Luca, I can't possibly accept this.'

'Of course you can. You're my wife and you have given me a beautiful son. Here, let me put it on.'

He bent his head to fasten the clasp around her wrist and Eve closed her eyes as his fingertips brushed against her skin, so warm and beguiling in contrast to the heavy, cold jewellery. Damn the bracelet, she thought. Throw it across the room and just touch me properly.

But he did not. He held her hand up and the brilliant circlet of jewels glittered, as if it were a trophy. Eve looked at it. It must have cost a fortune, and there were women who would have drawn blood for it, but she was not one of them.

'It's very beautiful,' she said dutifully.

The baby gave a little squawk and Luca almost seemed to expel a sigh of relief. 'I'll bring him to you.'

She watched him go to the carry-cot, her eyes drifting over the broad shoulders, the long, powerful legs and the way his dark hair curled slightly at the nape of his neck. The jeans stretched over the high, firm curve of his buttocks as he bent to lift the baby and she shivered with a hungry kind of longing. She hadn't exactly been immune to him before, but she had been preoccupied with the baby-to-be and with adjusting to life in a new city.

But now... Now all she wanted was to touch him. To rediscover the hard, strong lines of his face with her fingertips. To stroke them slowly over the silken flesh of his body.

She swallowed and turned appealing eyes up at him as Oliviero was placed warm and securely in her arms. 'You mustn't keep spoiling me like this. Honestly, Luca.'

'But I like doing it,' he said. And did it not simplify things? It had been so black and white when she had been pregnant. Thinking of her as a woman not yet recovered from the birth made it easier not to concentrate on the fact that no barrier now existed, and that they were just a man and a woman, living together. But not together.

Their eyes locked for long, confusing seconds and Eve felt a sudden tension which crackled through the room like electricity. Were they just going to ignore it, or endure it? And would it simply go away, or grow stronger and stronger?

'Luca—'

The baby wriggled restlessly and Luca knew he had to get away before he went back on everything he had vowed he would not do. 'Feed him,' he said shortly, and he didn't need to see the brief darkening of her eyes to know that he had hurt her.

CHAPTER THIRTEEN

THE soft, dark greens of the cypress trees painted umbrellas against the blue of the sky and the ancient stone walls passed by in a blur.

Eve leaned comfortably back in her seat and looked out at the countryside.

'All roads lead to Rome,' she said dreamily.

Luca gave a brief, satisfied smile. When had the change happened, he wondered, and when had he first started to notice it? He had watched her bloom and blossom, almost like watching a flower grow. And he had discovered that, just as a flower took time to blossom, change took time. You could not hurry it. Everything had its own rhythm. For a man used to clicking his fingers and getting exactly what he wanted, when he wanted, it had been a pretty major lesson in life.

'And all roads lead out of Rome, of course,' he murmured. 'As that's where we're headed!'

'Ha, ha!' She turned round and looked at Oliviero, who was peacefully asleep in his baby-seat. He was wearing a teeny little sailor-suit today—all crisp white cotton and embroidered anchors. Not quite what she would have chosen, but she had quickly discovered the Italian love of dressing their babies up, and she and Luca were driving out for a lunch party at Patricio and Livvy's country home and they had bought the outfit. 'He looks sweet, doesn't he?'

'He does indeed,' he said indulgently. *'Abbastanza buon mangiare.'*

'Which means?'

'Try and work it out.'

Eve frowned. She hadn't been learning Italian for long, but her progress had been remarkable, which she put down to Luca's tendencies as a slave-driver. *'Buon* means good.'

'Sì.'

The frown deepened. 'And I think *mangiare* is to eat.'

'It means, "good enough to eat".' He smiled and gave an exaggerated and very Latin shrug. 'You see? I can teach you nothing, Eve!'

But immediately she felt tension creep into the atmosphere and she didn't know whether she welcomed or cursed it. She was sure that there was plenty he could teach her, and she certainly wasn't thinking of the Italian language. So should she regard it as achievement or failure that she and Luca had managed to live together in relative harmony? As man and woman, if not man and wife.

How was it possible for them to communicate as friends and loving parents, and yet leave a great yawning hole in their communication about where their relationship was heading? And how long could it continue?

She stole a glance at Luca, who was swearing softly in Italian as a goat almost blundered into the road. He was just so gorgeous. He hated air-conditioning in cars, so had left his window half open and the warm, fragrant air blew in and ruffled his black hair. His shirt-sleeves were rolled up, showing the tiny dark hairs which sprinkled the strong arms, and the faded jeans emphasised the long, muscular definition of his thighs.

He was a hot-blooded and passionate man. She knew that for herself. She'd just had her six-week check-up following Oliviero's birth, and yet Luca had made no move towards her. How long could he continue to lead a life which was celibate? And it was one of those strange things—the longer it went on, the harder it would become to confront it.

Almost as if facing it would risk shattering the tentative trust and friendship they had built up together. And surely it was not her place to come out and say something? Was she living in fear that she might be rejected, or did it go deeper than that? For wasn't part of her terrified of the masquerade of having sex with Luca and pretending that it was just sex, when she had grown to love him so much and wanted nothing but his love in return?

And that was asking too much.

Luca turned his head, and smiled. 'Looking forward to lunch?'

She shifted slightly on her seat, afraid that he might be able to read the progression of her thoughts, half tempted to tell him to stop the car and then to hurl herself into his arms and see where *that* led them!

'Mmm. I like Patricio. And Livvy. I like all your friends.'

'Your friends too, now.'

'Yes.' But as friendships they were conditional, she knew that. They relied solely on her relationship with Luca and her position as his wife and sooner or later she was terrified that someone was going to discover just what a sham it all was. And then what?

Luca slowed the car down as it gingerly made its way down the bumpy lane, leading to a long, low farmhouse, sitting like a bird's egg in a glorious nest of green. Hens were scratching around by a barn door and, somewhere in the distance, Eve could hear a dove cooing.

Luca switched the engine off, his eyes roving over her as she undid her seat belt. She wore the simplest of outfits—a slim-fitting white denim skirt and a little T-shirt in jade green—and yet she managed to look like sex on legs. Thought maybe, he thought, subduing the familiar, dull ache—maybe that was more to do with his current state of heightened awareness. If she had worn a piece of all-enveloping sackcloth, he suspected that the end result of his thoughts would have been the same.

'You have got your figure back, *cara*,' he said softly. 'The outfit you wear looks lovely.'

Now why say something like *that*, just before they were due to go into lunch, or had that been the whole point? Pay her a compliment and make her aware of herself and leave her simmering and discontented throughout lunch? What the hell was he playing at?

'What, these old things?' she joked. 'Now, are you going to carry your son in, or shall I?'

The velvet-dark eyes glittered. 'Want to fight me for the pleasure?' he challenged softly.

Eve put her hand on the door-handle, afraid that he would see that it was shaking. Was he deliberately making everything he said absolutely *drip* with suggestive innuendo, or was that simply her interpretation of it?

'You can carry him,' she said quickly.

Everyone else had already arrived and were all

gathered beneath a vine-covered canopy. The adults were sitting down at a large, wooden trestle-table and various toddlers were waddling around on the terrace. It looked quite idyllic and perfect.

'Oh, doesn't it look peaceful?' sighed Eve longingly.

He looked at her profile, at the way her mouth had softened, and he nodded. 'The kind of way you thought Italy always should be?' he guessed softly.

She turned her head to look up at him. 'Kind of,' she admitted, but then voices were raised in welcome and there was no chance to say anything more.

Eve gave a wide smile, even though she couldn't really take in all the faces at first. But there was Patricio, and Livvy was getting to her feet and smiling a great smile of welcome.

'Eve! Luca! And Oliviero!'

Which gave the cue for everyone to scramble to their feet and coo over her darling baby, though Eve was acutely aware that the language switched immediately from Italian to English. And while she was working hard on it and knew that she couldn't possibly expect to become fluent overnight, she sometimes despaired of ever mastering the tongue with the careless ease which Luca and his friends had. But she would need to.

She didn't want to become one of those exiled mothers in a foreign land who never quite fitted in because they had never bothered to integrate. Or to have children who spoke a tongue which remained faintly foreign to her.

But thinking of the future like that scared her and so she forcefully put it out of her mind.

'Eve, come and sit down and have a drink,' said

Livvy. 'There are a few people here you don't know—let me introduce you.'

Eve accepted a glass of white wine and chewed on a salted almond as she was introduced to people with their impossibly romantic-sounding names— Claudio and Rosa, Caterina and Giacomo, Allessandro and Raimonda.

One woman in particular was just so beautiful that even the women seemed barely able to tear their eyes from her. Her name was Chiara, and she was younger than everyone else and with a man Eve hadn't seen before, either.

'Who is that woman?' she asked Luca softly as he positioned Oliviero in a quiet and shady spot.

Luca barely glanced over in the woman's direction. 'Her name is Chiara,' he said, in an odd kind of voice. 'And the man she is with is one of Italy's most famous film directors. She's an actress.'

Yes, she looked like an actress, Eve decided. She had met enough of them in her time. She had that way of holding herself which spoke of supreme confidence—but then who wouldn't be confident if they looked like that? Her glossy raven hair was knotted back in a French plait woven with ribbon and hung almost to the tiniest waist Eve had ever seen. She wore a simple dress in some kind of pinky-grey colour, but it moulded itself so closely to her body that no one could be in any doubt about what slender perfection lay beneath.

Eve helped herself to some salads and meats and began to falteringly attempt to speak a little Italian to Patricio, who laughed and teased her remorselessly. She drank wine and watched her husband as he kicked a ball to one of the little boys.

'Oh, Luca is just a frustrated footballer at heart,' shouted Patricio, and at that moment Luca looked up and met Eve's eyes and something inside her melted.

He wasn't just a frustrated footballer, but a frustrated lover, too, she thought. And so was she. And she wanted him. Desperately. All-consumingly. Someone had to put a stop to all this craziness and it might as well be her.

What could be the worst thing that could happen? That he would turn her down? No. That would not happen. She had seen the way he looked at her sometimes—he still wanted her, of that she was as certain as it was possible to be without actually testing it out.

So what was she really afraid of? That her love for him would grow deeper and deeper and never be reciprocated? And if so, wasn't that a pretty selfish way to view it?

Whatever. She wasn't going to hide from it any more. She was going to confront it, no matter how hurtful or painful. No matter what the outcome would be.

Livvy brought out a large chocolate cake to cheers from the men and greedy moans from the women, and only Chiara passed on the dessert.

'Go on—have a little,' tempted Livvy, but Chiara shook her head.

'But I have to wear tiny clothes.' She pouted and shrugged her tiny shoulders. 'It's how I earn my living!'

Eve had once read somewhere that men liked to see a woman eat—that it didn't matter what she did if they weren't around. Something about associating sex with hunger and that if a woman enjoyed her food, she would enjoy her body. If I were Chiara I would have taken a slice and played around with it, she thought. Until she remembered that she of all people was not in a position to hand out advice to anyone.

'Who wants to come and see my new horse?' asked Patricio.

'Oh, you men go and do your macho stuff,' said Livvy indulgently. 'We'll all just sit here and talk about you!'

'But we already know how wonderful we are!' swaggered her husband, and when she threw a cherry at him he caught it, and put it between his lips, biting on it, his eyes on his wife's mouth as he licked his tongue around the fruit and then slowly and deliberately threw the stone onto the grass.

Eve had to look away. How long since she had been intimate like that—*really* intimate? And if the truth were known, their sexual relationship had been so brief and intense that they had never slipped into that blissful state of being really comfortable with intimacy. She watched Luca go with a feeling of longing and suddenly she couldn't wait for the lunch to end.

'No more wine, thanks.' She shook her head. The unaccustomed alcohol and the warmth of the day had made her feel a little sleepy. Any minute now and she would doze off.

But then Oliviero woke and began to cry and Eve blinked and went over to pick him up. The little darling was damp with heat, despite the shade. She dropped a kiss on his head.

'Okay if I go inside and feed and change him?' she asked. 'It's cooler in there.'

'Sure.' Livvy smiled. 'I'll show you where.'

Eve settled herself in a shuttered and deliciously dark room. She fed Oliviero, then changed him, still marvelling at the size of his tiny little feet as she stroked her finger up and down the rosy soles.

She was just about to go back and join the others when Chiara came in.

'Hi!' Eve looked up and smiled. 'Too hot for you out there?'

Chiara smiled and shook her head as she ran a palm across her cool, sleek cheek. 'The sun doesn't touch me. I guess I'm used to it.'

Eve waited for Chiara to ask to hold the baby, but Chiara did not. Instead, she subjected Eve to a long and faintly puzzled scrutiny.

'You're English, aren't you?'

These were not good vibes, but Eve could cope— she had coped with enough women in the entertainment business to know how to handle women like Chiara.

'It's pretty obvious, isn't it?' She laughed politely but Chiara did not laugh back.

'You know,' Chiara said thoughtfully, 'you aren't really what we all expected—not at all the kind of woman we thought Luca would marry.'

Eve felt her heart begin to race. Suddenly her supposed ability to cope dissolved into a mass of insecurity. Keep it light-hearted, she told herself. Don't let her know it hurts.

'I think he rather surprised himself,' she said, but deep down she knew that this was vaguely dishonest. How triumphant would Chiara be if she knew the truth about their 'marriage'.

'You were pregnant, weren't you?'

Here it came. Just brazen it out. 'Yes, I was.'

Chiara nodded. 'It's a method which wouldn't work with a lot of men, but, of course, Luca was the perfect choice in more ways than one. He is far too much of a traditionalist to ever allow a child of his to be born out of wedlock.'

'I don't think this really is any of your business, do you?' asked Eve shakily, and hugged Oliviero to her, trying to concentrate on his sweet, baby smell and not the glitter of maliciousness in the actress's eyes.

But Chiara showed no signs of shutting up. 'I thought of trying it myself, if the truth be known.' She turned her huge chocolate-brown eyes up at Eve. 'But I left it too late and, by then, you had stepped in.'

'What are you talking about?'

Chiara smiled, as if she was enjoying herself immensely.

'Oh, didn't you know that I used to be Luca's lover?'

Eve's first reaction was to feel sick, until she told herself to grow up. He was bound to have had lots of lovers and they were bound to have been as beautiful as Chiara.

'No. No, I didn't.'

'In fact...' Chiara's manicured fingernails delved into her slim, neat handbag, and she pulled out a piece of newspaper '...this was the last photograph taken of us together. Would you like to see it?'

No, Eve would not like to see it, but she was not going to appear to be a totally-lacking-in-confidence kind of wife. She even managed a shrug. 'Why not?'

Because Eve was still holding the baby, Chiara

leaned over with the clipping and held it in front of her and Eve could smell the seductive musk of her fragrance.

'Here it is!'

If it had been any other couple, it would have been a pretty unremarkable photo, but it was not any other couple—it was Luca and Chiara. The beautiful people, thought Eve, slightly wistfully—with their jet-dark hair and olive skin and clothes which shrieked of wealth and success. Luca's eyes were narrowed at the camera. She knew that look—caught unawares and irritated. But Chiara was giving it everything she had—her hair tossed back and that big, mega-watt smile showing her perfect white teeth.

And then she noticed the date and her heart missed a beat.

It was the day...

It was the day after Lizzy's birthday.

The very same day that he had come round to Eve's house and tried to make love to her and she had very nearly let him. Dear God, he must have flown straight from her and into Chiara's arms!

In a way, she thanked God that she was holding onto Oliviero, for who knew what her reaction might have been otherwise? She guessed that she must have shown her horror and shock—she could feel all the blood draining from her face and she felt very slightly giddy.

But she somehow managed an equable smile.

'You make a lovely couple,' she said blandly.

It was clearly not the reaction that Chiara had expected, nor wanted. She put the clipping back in her bag.

'Yes,' she said, in an odd kind of voice. 'That's

what everyone said.' She sighed. 'It was a *wonderful* night. But then it was a wonderful relationship.'

Somehow Eve got through the rest of the afternoon, but she did it only by avoiding Luca's eyes wherever possible. She played with the children and she chatted animatedly with the adults, making sure that she was never on her own for him to come and speak to her, and making sure that her face bore a smile of enjoyment at all times.

Even in the car it was easy to maintain the masquerade. She didn't want a scene when he was driving, not with their son strapped in the back.

Luca frowned. 'Are you okay?'

Eve shut her eyes. 'I'm fine,' she said faintly. 'Just had a little too much sun and wine, I think.'

'Go to sleep, then,' he murmured. The powerful car purred along the rural roads and his eyes hardened as he stared ahead. Why the hell had Patricio invited Chiara? Her eyes had been following him round like some beaten puppy and he had felt sorry for the man who had been her companion.

Eve didn't sleep, just lay there, her mind going over and over it. There she had been, marvelling at Luca's restraint. Wondering why a man with such an overpowering sensuality had been able to suppress it.

Well, maybe he hadn't! Maybe that had all just been a ruse. What about the times when he had to slip out—to the shops or to his bank—was that all he was doing? Or was there some luscious lovely like Chiara, all too willing to give him what his wife was not?

Back at the apartment, she went through the motions of bathing and changing—refusing all Luca's offers of help—and she fed Oliviero in a simmering kind of silence.

Luca watched her, his antennae alerted to something, he didn't know what—but there was something about Eve's body language which told him that something was not right.

He waited until she had put the baby to bed, and then he looked up, noted the barely restrained fury on her face.

'So are you going to tell me what the problem is?'

'I should have thought that was perfectly obvious.'

'I am not going to conduct an entire conversation in riddles, Eve!' he snapped.

'Well, then.' She stared at him defiantly, hoping he wouldn't see the great oceans of despair in her eyes. '*I* am clearly the problem.'

He didn't react.

'Go on.'

It all came tumbling out then—all the hurt and longing and the feeling that she was here only because she had trapped him and that, in a way, she had trapped herself, and not just by having a baby. For she had come to learn that the love she felt was not returned, and how could she ever be happy knowing that? And that this might be the cleanest way to end it.

'You slept with Chiara the very day I refused to make love to you!' she accused. 'What happened, Luca? Did you get so stirred up that you had to do it with someone, anyone—that you had to do it with *her*!'

CHAPTER FOURTEEN

LUCA'S voice was like cold, deadly ice. 'Is that the opinion you have formed of me, then, Eve? A man so governed by his hormones that he is unable to control his sexual appetite? And surely if that were the case, then your theory contradicts itself—or no doubt I would have made more than one attempt to seduce you since you have been living here?'

Eve stared at him, her face warm with anger and confusion. Where was the remorse? The shame? The denial? 'What other explanation can there be?'

'Oh, I wonder,' he mocked sardonically.

Amid the hot fires of jealousy and the aching awareness that he had not so much as laid a finger on her since long before their marriage, Luca's look of disdain slowly began to seep into her fuddled brain and to make some kind of sense. She had judged him and found him wanting, choosing to believe the word of a woman she didn't know, without even giving him a chance to defend himself.

'So...you...you didn't?' Her voice sounded tiny, and the world seemed to hang on his answer.

He looked at her, and saw all the insecurity and fears written on her face. Had he been blind to them before? Or had he just chosen not to see? 'Of course I didn't,' he said softly. But he might have done, he supposed. A man less fastidious might have done. Or a man less blown away by an unknown woman in England who had turned him down...

'I guess I was angry that you wouldn't make love to me,' he admitted quietly. His arrogant sexual pride had suffered a wounding blow, but maybe it had needed to. 'Maybe even angrier with myself for having come on so strong.' He gave a half-smile. 'It's not my usual style, Eve.'

No, she couldn't imagine that he needed to.

He remembered back to what now seemed like a lifetime ago, but, of course, it was. 'I told myself that you meant nothing and so, yes, I agreed to see Chiara that night. I suspect that she tipped off the photographers, because when we came out of the restaurant the paparazzi were there. But nothing happened. I dropped her off and I went home. Alone.'

'So why did she say those things?'

'Because she wants me. Because she's jealous of you.'

'Of *me*?' said Eve, in an empty little voice. If only she realised what little there was to be jealous of. 'She said you'd had a wonderful relationship.'

'We had a brief affair—that was all.'

'Which is what ours should have been,' she pointed out painfully. 'Shouldn't it?'

He stared at her, realising how important his next words were. Realising that the truth could hurt, but that didn't mean you should avoid it. 'Who knows?' he said softly. 'No one can see into the future and no one can change the past. But that wasn't the way it turned out, was it, Eve? Things happened. Fate stepped in. We had a baby—'

'And we got married,' she finished. 'A...farce of a marriage.'

'Is that what you think it is?'

'Well, isn't it?'

'It isn't the marriage I want it to be, no,' he said carefully.

'You mean you want us to start having sex?'

He gave a bitter laugh. 'Are you trying to shock me, *cara*? Or anger me? Do you want to enrage me with your bold, flip comments so that I come over there and kiss you and take your clothes off and pull you to the floor and make love to you?' He saw the sudden dull flush which darkened her cheeks and he felt an answering ache which almost tore him in two. 'Oh,' he said softly. 'So you do.'

'Luca,' she said huskily and her tongue snaked out to circle her lips, like a hungry little animal. 'Yes. Yes, of course I want that. Don't you?'

He felt so close to acting out his words that he had to resist the desire with every ounce of self-restraint he possessed.

'No! No, I don't!'

She stared at him in hurt and confusion. This was the rejection she had always feared, but maybe it had been a long time coming. And maybe she needed to know. You couldn't keep hiding from your feelings just because you were afraid they might hurt you. Being mature meant having the courage to confront the real issues.

She stared at him, her voice shaking, willing herself not to cry. 'What, then? What is it that you want, Luca?'

He could talk around it for hours. Quantify and justify and explain it, but in the end there was only one thing he needed to tell her. 'I need to tell you that I love you, Eve,' he said huskily. '*Ti amo*. I love you so very much.'

Eve bit her lip. 'Please don't say that.'

'Why?' His voice was gentle. 'Don't you want me to love you?'

What had she just thought about having courage? 'Yes.'

It was such a soft whisper of a word that he barely heard it. 'Say that again, Eve.'

'Yes. Yes.' She turned her eyes up to him. 'Yes, of course I want you to love me as I love you, but I've wanted it for so long that I'm scared you don't mean it.'

'Oh, I mean it,' he said. 'But this is all new stuff to me, Eve. I have never said it before. Never felt it before.'

For a moment she saw vulnerability written on his face. 'What, never?'

He shook his head and now the aching within him became more than physical. For the first time in his life he felt a great, gaping emotional hole which only Eve could fill. '*Tesora*—'

The haunting, heartfelt term of endearment broke through every last barrier and she crossed the distance between them, only a little distance really, but it felt like the divide between the old life and the new.

'Luca. Dear, darling, sweetest Luca.'

He pulled her into his arms, kissed the top of her head and then tipped her face up to look at his and her green-grey eyes were huge. He saw the tears on her cheeks and he brushed them away with his lips.

'Never cry, *tesora*,' he whispered against her skin. 'Promise me you will never cry again.'

She shook her head. 'I can't promise you that,' she said shakily. 'We might have rows—fierce, terrible rows—and you might make me cry—'

'And will you make me cry, too?' he teased softly.

'You? A big man like you. *Crying?*' But her words faded to nothing when she saw the brightness in his dark eyes and in that moment she saw his vulnerability too and her hug became fierce and she was overwhelmed with love for him. 'Luca,' she whispered. 'Oh, Luca, *please.*'

He knew what she wanted and what he wanted, too. He had waited too long and he could wait no longer. Without another word he picked her up into his arms and carried her into his bedroom.

'I want to see you naked,' he said shakily. He unbuttoned the white skirt and let it fall to her feet. *'Cielo dolce,'* he murmured indistinctly. 'For too many nights have I dreamed of you like this.'

She felt his warm hands on her hips and she felt so dizzy with desire she thought that she might faint. 'I...I know. I've dreamed of it, too.'

'Undress me,' he urged as he slid a delicate little pair of panties down her legs, his fingertips brushing against the silkenness of her thighs and feeling her shiver beneath them.

'I...I...can't,' she breathed helplessly. 'I can barely think, nor breathe, nor feel...' But he took her hand and guided it to his heart.

'Can you feel that?'

The strong, powerful thunder of his blood. Her head fell to his shoulder. 'Yes.' She shuddered against him. 'Oh, yes.'

'That is for you, *cara mia*. All and only for you. Now lift your arms,' he instructed gently, as he would a child, and obediently she did as he said, so that he pulled the T-shirt off and tossed it away, snapping the clasp of her bra open so that her breasts fell free and unfettered. He wanted to take one into his mouth, to suckle and to tease it, but a need even stronger drove him on.

Ruthlessly, he stripped the clothes from his body until they were both naked and then he drew her down onto the bed, smoothing the hair away from her face, looking deep into her eyes.

Luca sighed. 'I want you. So very much.'

There was a split-second silence. 'Then kiss me.'

'I will kiss you until you beg me to kiss you no more,' he promised. But still he gazed at her, as if wanting to prolong this moment, this mind-shattering realisation of all that she had come to mean to him.

Eve lifted her mouth. 'Don't make me wait any more,' she moaned.

He kissed her back, feeling her fingers slide with abandon over his skin as if she was relearning his body by touch alone. 'Greedy woman,' he laughed, with soft delight.

He felt as though there were a million new nerve endings in his body. She could thrill him by the soft whisper of her lips, make him tremble with the wet touch of her tongue. He shuddered, helpless beneath her and then he moved above her and made his mouth move along the moist, erotic pathways of her skin until she cried out.

And when he entered her, he said her name and it was as if he had never made love before—the way people spoke of, but he had never believed could happen. Not to him. A complete communion, he thought dazedly. Afterwards he lay back and stared at the ceiling with eyes which felt new and reborn. 'Oh, Eve,' was all he said.

Eve kissed his elbow. It was a particularly gorgeous elbow. Then she clambered on top of him, her hair spilling untidily all over, some of it on his face, so that he laughed and blew it away.

'Luca?'

'Mmm?'

'How long have you loved me for?'

He picked up another errant strand and thoughtfully twirled it around his finger. 'Honestly?'

'Honestly.'

'If you want me to give you a time and a date, then I cannot,' he admitted. 'It kind of crept up on me. Like being out in the rain. A little drop at first, here and there, so faint that you thought you might have imagined it. And then a little more, and then more still—until suddenly I was standing in a deluge without quite realising how I'd got there!'

She pretended to pout. 'So I'm like a storm?'

'Mmm. Wild and strong and overwhelming.'

'But you knew that I loved you?'

He smiled. It had happened to him too often in his life not to. And as always the realisation had scared him, but this time for very different reasons—not because he wanted to run away from her love, but because he had to be sure he was worthy of it. It would have been easier to have been impetuous, but, caught up in these new and strange emotions, he had used caution. 'Yes, *cara*,' he said softly. 'I knew.'

'And when were you going to get around to telling me you loved me back?' she persisted. 'How long would you have waited? What if we hadn't had that row today—then I would never have known.'

'Oh, yes, you would. I suppose I was waiting for the right moment only, when it happened, it was a wrong moment, really. Not champagne and flowers but a misunderstanding over a jealous woman.'

Eve wriggled luxuriously against him. 'But it brought things to a head.' She yawned.

'Mmm.' He idly put her little finger in his mouth and sucked on it. 'You see, we have done everything the wrong way round, *cara*. At first there was passion and only passion, but before we knew it there was a baby, too.'

'And anger,' she ventured.

He nodded. 'And anger. But no getting to know you. No old-fashioned courtship. No getting to know each other. No trust built nor friendship established. I wanted that and you deserved no less than that— we needed that if we were to share our future.'

It was, she realised, a very matter-of-fact way of looking at it, but she didn't mind. And really—when you thought about it—it made sense. For marriage was a contract as well as a love affair.

'So this,' she said as a glorious thought occurred to her. 'This is really our honeymoon?'

'It sure is.' He smoothed the flat of his hand over her bottom.

'And...and how long will it last?'

'How does for ever sound?' he questioned huskily as his mouth moved down to cover hers.

EPILOGUE

THE afternoon sun was soft and so was the warm breeze which ruffled the hair of the two women as they sat watching the children play.

'Oh, Eve,' sighed Lizzy. 'This is just so-o-o beautiful.'

Eve looked around her, trying to see it through her friend's eyes, recalling her gasp of joy when Luca had first brought her here.

The house in Viale Monte Pincio was up in the mountains outside Rome and only an hour-and-a-half drive away from the city, but it was like being in another world. The entrance to the garden was through a tall, wrought-iron gate and there was an abundance of pine trees and bay bushes and many fruits growing there. Blackcurrant, raspberries, lemon and cherries.

'Yes,' she agreed quietly. 'So very beautiful.'

On the grass, among the daisies, Kesi played with Oliviero. Luca and Michael had gone to find some cool drinks while Eve and Lizzy were sitting idly watching them, listening to the buzz of the bees and the call of the birds.

'You're so happy,' Lizzy observed.

'How could I not be?' said Eve simply. 'I feel like I've come home.'

She and Luca had both come round to the way of thinking that maybe the apartment wasn't the best place for Oliviero to grow up in. They had decided to buy a house in the city itself, but more and more they came here, to this quiet, rural retreat. For the first time in his life Luca was taking time out to smell the roses. And the coffee. And proving to be the most hands-on father that Eve could ever have wished or hoped for.

'And Luca doesn't miss his apartment?'

'Not at all.' Eve shook her head. 'Actually, he was the one who brought up the subject about moving. We talked about it and decided that, lovely as it is, it wasn't really a family home.'

Lizzy sat up, which wasn't easy as she was pregnant and lying in a deckchair. 'You don't mean you're having another baby?' she questioned excitedly.

Eve giggled. 'No. Not yet. Maybe not for a while yet.' She and Luca adored their son with all their hearts but knew that another pregnancy would bring about another change and felt that they had had quite enough change for the time being! They were enjoying their life, their son and their love. They were content to wait. And see.

'And you don't miss working?' Lizzy questioned.

Eve shook her head. 'Not a bit. Luca has friends in the television industry over here and, now that my Italian is quite passable, it wasn't inconceivable that I could get a job in the business again—maybe editing or producing. *Grazie, il mio uomo piccolo*!' This to Oliviero who had just tottered up and planted a battered daisy in his mother's lap, before tottering off again. 'But I didn't want to,' she finished. 'Luca is around a lot and I...well, I love motherhood. I love being a wife. Luca's wife. Who could ask for anything more?'

'Not even a drink, *il mio angelo*?' questioned the deep silken voice behind her which always had the power to make her shiver with longing.

She smiled up at him. 'Oh, I think I could probably manage a drink!'

Michael flopped down on a deckchair and Luca put the tray down before sinking to the grass, leaning his head lazily against Eve's knees, and she ruffled his hair as she so loved to.

'It seems a long way from the Hamble,' observed Lizzy sleepily.

'A long way from anywhere. It's just so peaceful,' yawned her husband. 'Well, you're both very lucky, I must say.'

Luca glanced up at Eve and their eyes met in a long, precious moment. Yes, they were lucky enough to have the money to buy them houses in Italy, and to keep Eve's on back in England, too. But the luckiest thing was to have found each other. It didn't matter where they lived—they could make anywhere their home, just as long as they were together.

For they had both discovered that a relationship didn't have to have a perfect beginning to have the perfect ending.

Even more passion for your reading pleasure...

Escape into a world of intense passion and scorching
romance! You'll find the drama, the emotion, the
international settings and happy endings that you've
always loved in Harlequin Presents. But we've turned up
the thermostat just a little, so that the relationships really
sizzle.... Careful, they're almost too hot to handle!

This September, in

TAKEN FOR
HIS PLEASURE
by Carol Marinelli
(#2566)...

Sasha ran out on millionaire Gabriel Cabrini—
and he has never forgiven her. Now he wants
revenge.... But Sasha is determined not to
surrender again, no matter how persuasive
he may be....

**Also look for MASTER OF PLEASURE (#2571)
by bestselling author Penny Jordan.
Coming in October!**

www.eHarlequin.com

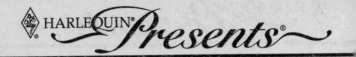

Legally wed, but he's never said... "I love you."

They're

Wedlocked!

Where
marriages are
made in haste...
and love
comes later....

Three years ago Kayla removed billionaire Duardo Alvarez's
wedding ring.... Now desperate circumstances have forced
Kayla to ask him for help. But Duardo's price is high:
marry him again, or he'll walk away....

Buy this book for the full story!

PURCHASED BY THE BILLIONAIRE
by Helen Bianchin

Book #2563, on sale September 2006

And if you like this miniseries, look out for another
Wedlocked! marriage story coming to you in October:

THE MILLIONAIRE'S LOVE-CHILD
by Elizabeth Power (Book #2577)

Dinner at 8...
Don't be late!

He's suave and sophisticated,
He's undeniably charming.
And above all, he treats her like a lady.

But don't be fooled....

Beneath the tux, there's a primal passionate
lover, who's determined to make her his!

Wined, dined and swept away by a British billionaire!